Roxy Buckles
AND THE CRY OF THE FALCON

Published in Canada by Engen Books, Chapel Arm, NL.

A CIP catalogue record for this book is available from Library and Archives Canada.

Print: 978-1-77478-183-8
eBook: 978-1-77478-193-7

Distributed by:
Engen Books
www.engenbooks.com
submissions@engenbooks.com

First mass market paperback printing: June 2025

Cover Design: Ellen Curtis
Cover Image: Kate Cunningham

Roxy Buckles
AND THE CRY OF THE FALCON

NICOLE LITTLE

For Kashi.

CHAPTER ONE

Roxy strutted into the office on four-inch stilettos, her short butter-yellow sundress swirling in a cloud around her thighs as the automatic doors whooshed shut behind her, stirring up an errant breeze. It had just gone 8 o'clock. The morning was bright and clear; the sort of day that invited open windows and optimism. She slid a pair of leopard print cat eye sunglasses atop her head, where they rested amongst her mop of golden curls, and winked broadly at the woman behind the main desk of Buckles & Associates.

"Surprise!"

"Roxy," Suki squealed in delight. "You're here!"

"In the flesh," Roxy replied, grinning, one hand on her hip. She sashayed her way closer to the desk, bent down and wrapped her arms around Suki in a tight hug, pressing a kiss to the top of her head as she rose. "I've missed you, my friend."

"And I, you," Suki replied, reaching out to grab Roxy's hand. She gave it a firm squeeze. "I'm so glad you're back. Maybe things can finally start getting back to normal now."

A giggle erupted from Roxy, and Suki shot her a look. "When have things around here ever been *normal*?"

Roxy found herself reaching for the pile of pink missed call slips stacked haphazardly at the corner of the desk. She quirked an eyebrow. "And I see not much else has changed in my absence?"

"You got that right." Suki rolled her eyes, laughing. "I'm just a little less worried about one of us being murdered in our beds."

Roxy had enjoyed her time on Mauw but she was incredibly happy to be back on Aurora. The pull she felt, that familiar call to action that had laid dormant for so many months, was now returning full force. It felt damn good.

Being idle, it just wasn't for Roxy.

She sifted through the massive pile of messages and job requests as she made her way across the room to the inner office. She stopped mid-stride as a familiar name stared out at her in neat, precise handwriting: Ethel-Beth Lester. Her eyes widened and she looked up at Suki, waving the slip of paper. "Seriously?"

Suki shrugged. "Like I said, nothing ever changes."

Roxy placed the slip beneath the pile and shook her head in consternation. She would most definitely deal with that one later. Then, brow knitted, she began to count: one, two, three… *twelve* messages in total from Hadrien Durand, Acting Commander of The Planetary Regulation Committee.

"They've been calling non-stop," Suki said, watching her. "I finally just stopped writing it down."

Roxy turned and shook her head, exasperation written all over her face. "What could there be to discuss? Hours and hours of depositions and interviews already. I gave my statement that night. There's nothing left to talk about." She crumpled the slips of paper into a small, tight ball and tossed it effortlessly into the trash bin.

"Nice shot!"

"At least one of us is," Roxy teased with a playful smirk.

"Hey," Suki Kwan replied indignantly, "It was dark. And he was moving a lot. And it was really far away. I tried my best. Carmine should be counting his lucky stars that I *am* such a lousy shot."

"Excuses, excuses." Roxy threw back her head and laughed. "I'm sorry, Suki, but you really won't ever live this down."

"Whatever," Suki muttered, but Roxy saw her lips twitch as she struggled to suppress a smile.

A sharp trill sounded from Suki's desk, interrupting their easy-going conversation. Suki's eyes glanced from the display on the com and then back to Roxy's curious face. "It's Durand's office... again." She held her breath and waited for a response from Roxy.

Roxy exhaled loudly through her nostrils and threw her hands up in defeat. "Fine. Just send the call through. I'll have to deal with it sooner or later. Might as well do it now when I'm *relaxed*. But you and I," she pointed at Suki. "We'll talk later. I want to

know everything that happened while I was away."
She squared her shoulders and stalked through the
door to her office, slamming it shut behind her.

Suki snorted. With the tap of a button, she grate-
fully transferred the call through to Roxy. She
chewed on the inside of her cheek, lost in thought as
she picked up a piece of paper. She crumpled it into a
ball, eyed the trash bin, aimed and fired. "Dammit."
She sighed as the ball bounced off the rim and landed
on the floor. "At least I took out a kneecap," she muttered to herself. "Better than nothing at all."

***

Roxy took another deep breath and then, despite
feeling woefully unprepared, accepted the call. "Roxy
Buckles speaking."

"Ms. Buckles. What a pleasure to finally speak
with you." The warm deep voice reverberated down
the communication line.

"My apologies, Acting Commander Durand, I
have been… away. My location was quite remote."

"Understandable, Ms. Buckles, no need to apolo-
gize. We all need to go off the grid every once in a
while." Roxy heard a smile in his voice. "I promise
I won't keep you long. I know that we have taken
up enough of your time already. The reason for my
call… I was hoping to speak with you. In person. At
your convenience, of course. It's rather important."

Roxy muted the call so that he could not hear the
unbridled cursing at her end and when she'd tired
herself out, she sighed, regretful that she had tak-

en the call to begin with. She'd seen enough of The PRC Plaza to last several lifetimes, and the thought of walking into those offices once again made her stomach churn unpleasantly. She wanted to wipe her hands clean of the whole lot of them.

As though sensing the reason behind her hesitation and silence, Durand interjected with an offer: "I would be happy to meet on neutral territory if you would prefer. Lunch perhaps? My treat."

This was virtually unheard of. A PRC official having lunch off-site with a mere mortal such as herself? You went to them. They never came to you. Curiosity piqued, Roxy quickly unmuted the conversation. "Yes, that would work for me."

"Excellent," he replied, sounding quite like he actually *did* think it was excellent. "I will have Mordean, my assistant, blip you the details shortly. I look forward to making your acquaintance."

"Thank you, Acting Commander. I look forward to meeting you as well." Roxy ended the call and leaned back, allowing the chair to recline as she pursed her lips and contemplated what the Acting Commander could possibly have to discuss with her. Her wristlet emitted a short beep and Roxy shook her head in surprise at the prompt message. A *SkyShaw* would be there to pick her up at noon.

Well, she thought to herself, *guess I'll find out soon enough.*

CHAPTER TWO

Suntwin was at its zenith in the sky as Roxy swiped her access card, stepped through the front doors of The Chaffey Building, and onto the street outside. Security was a little tighter these days – no one got in or out without clearance.

Narrowly avoiding a collision with a speeding turbo-courier on a Zip-Board, she muttered a curse under her breath, flipped her sunglasses down onto her nose and checked the time on her wristlet. As the alarm chimed the noon hour, the *SkyShaw* pulled to a stop a short distance away. They were nothing if not punctual. Roxy felt her lips curl into a genuine smile as she stepped inside the carriage.

Roxy found herself being whisked away from the central core and the bustling chaos of the big city, past the calmness of Suburbia and directly into the Boho District. A haven for artists and creatives, it was peppered with small artisan establishments, musical venues and retro diners reminiscent of those found on Earth in the Twenty-First Century.

The *SkyShaw* driver refused her payment, stating

the ride had already been taken care of, and released the mechanism that held the doors closed. Roxy disembarked near a brightly lit restaurant, the sign outside indicating she was about to enter the *Out of this World Eatery* which proclaimed to be a *Purveyor of Authentic Earthside Cuisine*. A cheerful tune played over the loudspeaker and a servo-bot bopped past Roxy on what she thought might have been an old pair of roller skates as she made her way to the podium with a sign that read: *Please wait to be seated.*

"Well, hey there, darlin', what can I do for you on this fine day?" drawled the young man who scurried over when he saw her standing there. He was wearing a purple vest and a bright pink bow tie. She liked him instantly.

Roxy smiled, hesitant, not sure exactly what the protocol was here in an Earthside diner. "I'm meeting someone for lunch?"

"Say no more, sweetheart. Y'all just follow me and I will bring you straight to your table." He winked at Roxy and turned with a flourish.

The snappy young host led Roxy to a cherry-red booth in a quiet corner away from the hustle and bustle of the restaurant. Hadrien Durand rose from where he had been seated and extended his hand in greeting, his clasp warm and firm. He was slightly shorter than her, a fact exacerbated by Roxy's four-inch heels. His close-cropped dark hair was flecked with gray but his demeanor was youthful and the laugh lines at his eyes and mouth suggested a man who smiled and laughed often. He indicated the seat across from him and Roxy slid onto the worn plastic seat.

"A server will be right with you. Now you have yourselves a lovely meal." The host gave a cheery wave and headed back behind the bar, where he promptly picked up a book in one hand and a coconut with a straw in the other.

"Ms. Buckles, so glad you could join me." Durand grinned and handed her a menu. "This is my favorite place to eat in all of Aurora. I come here often. I highly recommend the *fries*. It was a very popular snack food on Earth."

Roxy smiled in response but was suddenly struck by the absurdity of the situation. She felt awkward, like she was on a first date. She examined the menu while her mind frantically tried to come up with something to say that didn't make her sound like a complete tool.

"Ah," Durand exclaimed, "here she comes. My apologies, but I took the liberty of ordering us a drink. Something called a *milkshake*. Another of Earth's favorites or so I have been told."

The waitress lackadaisically plunked two large frosty glasses on the table and walked away without a word.

"Isn't it wonderful?" Durand took a big pull of his drink and closed his eyes in abject pleasure. "Try it." His exuberance was contagious and Roxy, who was beginning to think herself no longer capable of making conversation, slipped the concoction closer and took a tentative sip. Flavor exploded on her tongue and Durand laughed at the expression on her face. "Told you it was good. It's a flavor called chocolate."

She swallowed, took a deep breath and plunged in headfirst. "Acting Commander Durand, forgive me for being forward – it's not that I do not appreciate your hospitality or this lovely drink – but I have to admit that I am more than a little curious as to why you have invited me here."

The waitress appeared suddenly at their table. Durand turned to her with a smile. "We will have a large order of your *fries* please. Oh, and some of that sauce that usually comes with it – the red one. We'll have two of those."

"You got it," she replied dryly, and strolled away.

"Please excuse me, Ms. Buckles." He flushed. "But I skipped breakfast this morning and now I'm famished. Now, to answer your question…" He leaned forward, his dark eyes crinkling at the corners. "By the end of this week I will no longer be *Acting* Commander. I will take over the position fully. I will continue to try and repair the damage done by Seth Carmine and his followers."

"Congratulations," Roxy exclaimed. "I am confident that you will be able to do just that." Roxy had done her research; Hadrien Durand was more than qualified for the job. He had more commendations and awards for bravery than Roxy thought possible for any one person.

"Thank you. I appreciate the vote of confidence."

He continued, "My first order of business will be rebuilding The Academy. Tomorrow, crews will go in and clear away the debris. We will start with a clean slate. What Aurora needs now is a new generation of dependable lawmakers and teachers; we need to earn back the trust of our people."

Roxy nodded. "I couldn't agree more."

"I am glad to hear you say that." Durand smiled like the cat that ate the canary. "Because I want you to come and work alongside me. Be my Lieutenant. I am positive that together the two of us can set things right again."

Roxy stared at him, dumbfounded. She quickly closed her mouth; she hadn't even realized it had been hanging open.

"Fries." Roxy startled as the waitress plopped a large platter in the middle of the Formica table. "Enjoy."

Lieutenant Buckles, Roxy thought to herself as her hand edged towards the plate of food, the enticing aroma of the fried delicacy too hard to resist. *Has a nice ring to it.*

CHAPTER THREE

"Well, what are you going to do?" Suki stared at her in wide-eyed wonder, practically salivating over the juicy gossip, as Roxy dished animatedly on the meeting with Durand, leaving out no details. "No, don't tell me. You *have* to do this. It's basically your dream job. There's no question about it."

"I... I'm not sure what I'm going to do about it, to be honest. I have worked really, really hard to build Buckles & Associates up, to make it a successful business and to get it to the point where it is today. I know I don't want to give that up. Plus, I've just gotten back to work, I don't want to leave again so soon." She laughed, though it was without humor. "I can't expect to have it all now, can I?"

"And why not?" Suki demanded, hitting her palm against the desktop. "Who says you can't have it all? And if anyone does tell you that, I will kick their ass. I have seen you accomplish the impossible over the years, Roxy Buckles, and I won't stand by while you pass this up."

"Suki, come on. Be reasonable."

"Why are you so god damn stubborn, Roxy?" Suki's nostrils flared. "Why are you so afraid to accept help? Because that's the problem here isn't it? You'd have to give up a modicum of control over this place," Suki spread her arms wide to encompass the office. "And you can't bring yourself to do it."

Frowning, Roxy crossed her arms across her chest. "I'm afraid I don't know what you're talking about." As soon the words left her mouth, Roxy realized that she knew full well exactly what Suki was talking about. That didn't mean she was ready to admit it. Old habits die hard.

Suki wrinkled her nose. "You're stuck in this mind set. You slipped right back into it the minute you arrived back in Aurora. I knew you would. You know, just because you *can* do everything yourself, doesn't mean that you *have to*. There are people who love you and want to help... you just have to let them." She was out of breath, but she'd only just started. She raised her hand as Roxy opened her mouth, retort upon her lips. "No, no, let me finish before I lose my nerve here. Look, I know I'm a terrible shot – shut up! – but I can do so much more around here: the smaller jobs; I can gather information and follow up on leads, I can do interviews or run interference. Just let me try. River can help too; I know they'd jump at the chance to spend more time here on Aurora. And I can name at least ten more people who would kill for the opportunity to work for you. Take a step back from this for a little while." She gestured again around the room. "The PRC has always been your dream. Go get it."

Leaning over, Suki reached into a desk drawer to pull out a bottle of high-end red label hibiscus champagne. "Now, I've been saving this fancy schmancy thing for a very special occasion." With a flourish she popped open the bottle and raised it towards Roxy in a toast: "To *Lieutenant* Buckles; the galaxy won't know what hit it!"

She took a gulp, coughed and waved a hand in front of her face before pressing her fingers to her mouth. "Oh shit, how can something so expensive taste so horrible?" She passed the bottle to Roxy, shaking her head. "Your turn. Bottoms up."

Roxy laughed and took a swig, grimacing as the warm sickly-sweet bubbles flooded her mouth. She swallowed instinctively and gave a small shudder. The milkshake had been much better.

Suki was right.

Deep down, Roxy knew that she *was* ridiculously stubborn and especially hard-headed about accepting help; her childhood had made sure of that. *Dammit*, Roxy thought to herself, *if I admit this, I will never live it down*. Yes, Suki was right about a lot of things; maybe the past ten years might have been a whole hell of a lot different if Roxy had been listening to her friend from the start.

Roxy gritted her teeth and took another tentative sip of the sparkling alcohol, hoping that the first gulp might have prepared her better for the second. Alas, it was not to be. The champagne really was that terrible. Something else Suki was right about. She'd be insufferable if Roxy ever told her.

Roxy leaned forward and passed the bottle back to her friend. "I guess we're committed to drinking this now, hey? Can't waste it."

Suki groaned and eyed the champagne with trepidation before drinking from it again. She turned to Roxy who had suddenly gone quiet. "What? Roxy, what's wrong?"

Leaning a hip against the desk, her brow furrowed and her lips pursed in thought, Roxy had been struck by a sudden flash of brilliance. "Absolutely nothing. In fact, things might just be going right for a change." She grinned. "How does *Buckles & Kwan Incorporated* sound to you?"

CHAPTER FOUR

Six months later.

Roxy flicked the Zip to autopilot, shrugged out of her jacket, and hunkered down for a well-deserved kip in the small space behind the seats. It was claustrophobic at best, but Roxy, by necessity, could fall asleep anywhere.

This last job had taken her closer to Earth than she cared for. A far too lengthy excursion for what turned out to be a simple problem. Now she was traveling across a large expanse of space, with nothing but the drone of the ship and her own thoughts to keep her company. She liked neither of those two things.

An incessant chirp penetrated the fog of exhaustion. Roxy was slow to wake. Her hand grasped the pilot's chair as she pulled herself to standing. Roxy reached out, still half-blind with sleep, to silence the alarm on the Zip's luminescent control panel. Her hand froze above the button. She frowned.

It wasn't an alarm at all.

It was a distress signal.

***

Roxy's brow furrowed in confusion. A distress signal in the middle of nowhere, with no other ships visible on the radar, no known planets nearby. It was unheard of.

She was no longer tired. And there was really only one thing left for Roxy to do. She was going to follow that signal and find out what the hell was going on.

***

Bleary eyes scanned the expanse of open space for a light, a ship, or any clue to what she might be looking for. The signal had grown faint – she'd been following the sound of the blip for hours and felt no closer to solving the mystery. She yawned, on the verge of giving up.

The Zip gave a violent jerk. Roxy slammed forward into the console, breath rushing from her lungs in a whoosh. The ship shuddered and dropped so quickly that Roxy had no time to attempt evasive measures. Alarms blared, the voice of the automatic system shouted *too low, too low, pull up, pull up,* drowning out the flow of obscenities from Roxy.

She was about to go down with the ship.

***

The Zip barrel rolled. Roxy clung to her seat.

Too low. Terrain. Too low. Terrain. Too low. Terrain, the robotic voice shrieked repeatedly.

The nauseating roll came to an abrupt end as the ship slammed into a rocky outcrop before tumbling down the side of a cliff. Roxy's head smashed into the steering column; she felt a gush of warmth flow down the side of her face. "But... this isn't supposed to be here," was her last coherent thought before the unwelcome cloak of darkness folded her in its embrace.

***

A low murmur penetrated the fog of oblivion that shrouded Roxy. She struggled to focus in the low light. She was no longer in the Zip.

She attempted to sit up. A firm hand on her shoulder held her back.

"Please don't move. You have a nasty head injury."

The quiet voice was soothing. Roxy sank back against the soft surface.

"Where am I?" she croaked, wincing against the jackhammer in her head. Then she remembered: the search, the crash. She repeated the question again, firmly this time.

"Where am I?" Then, "Who are you?"

"I am Brie Nova. I was hoping you yourself might be able to answer the first part of your question. We have been unable to ascertain our location."

"Who is we?" Roxy brushed away the hand that still rested on her shoulder and sat up. She gaped in surprise. She was inside a large, long, oval-shaped ship. A woman sat next to her. Her close-cropped hair was flaming red, her eyes curious, her face kind but guarded as she gazed at Roxy.

Taking a deep breath, she said, "I am Captain Brie Nova of *The HMS Falcon*, a Seeker from Earth. I'm not sure exactly how long ago we crashed here but our cryo-pods appear to have begun opening a few weeks ago. Mind telling us who you are?"

Roxy looked around, assessing. There were about a dozen people gathered at the far end of the room; they appeared to be from all walks of life.

"I'm Roxy Buckles. Is this everyone?" she asked, one of a million questions she had buzzing around in her head.

"There are thirteen of us here in this room." She turned to the woman standing hesitantly nearby. "This is Major Ingrid Van Wyk, my second-in-command."

The woman stepped forward. "We started out with two hundred, though many seem to have perished in the accident. Some of the cryo-pods still remain sealed and functioning." Her softly accented voice lowered. "For now, anyway."

"You said, a Seeker?" Roxy questioned. Her head throbbed viciously. This whole thing felt like a fever dream.

The woman nodded. "Yes, a ship sent out by The Relocation Board in search of other hospitable planets conducive to human life."

Roxy shook her head. "I'm not aware of any such program and I work for The PRC. I would know," she challenged.

The captain's nose crinkled in confusion. "PRC?"

Roxy sighed. "The Planetary Regulation Committee. It oversees all the... how do you not know this?"

The people across the room began to talk amongst themselves while glancing apprehensively at Roxy.

"I have never heard of such a thing," Brie replied. "Just how hard did you hit your head, Ms. Buckles?"

"I'm beginning to wonder the same thing," Roxy muttered. She fell silent, thinking. "When did you leave Earth?" she suddenly asked.

"Well, The Relocation Board was established just after The Great Interstellar Blip and within months, the Seekers were launched…" The look on Roxy's face made her falter. "Ma'am, you have gone very pale."

"That's just not possible," Roxy whispered, her mind working frantically. "But… there's no other explanation."

"Ms. Buckles?" Brie, perplexed, placed a hand tentatively on Roxy's knee. "Are you okay?"

Roxy took a deep breath. "I don't know how to tell you this, Captain Nova, but The Great Interstellar Blip that you speak of…"

"Yes," Brie prompted as Roxy paused.

"I learned about that in school. In history class, to be exact. You see, The Blip *is* a part of history. Because it happened nearly 100 years ago."

CHAPTER FIVE

"Alright, listen: Roxy is missing."

"Wha–"

"Don't interrupt me," Suki admonished. "Meet me at Roxy's condo. I'm setting up a home base there."

"Who–"

But she had already disconnected.

The conversation went much the same as Suki reached out to the list of people she had procured; a list of Roxy's friends, others that could help. To the last one she added, "Bring food."

***

The low buzz of conversation halted immediately as Suki stood, leaning on her cane. CoCo or the Condo-Comm Interface had been engaged (Suki had bypassed Roxy's password very easily – she used the same one for everything) and the wall in front of them was a vast display of maps and charts projected by the electronic assistant.

"Thank you all for coming."

"As if we had a choice," a young girl muttered under her breath.

Suki shot her a withering glance that silenced her instantly.

"Roxy is missing." She gestured towards the map on the wall. "The last known coordinates for the Zip are indicated in red. It went off the radar at approximately nineteen hundred hours, three days ago. The backup transponder went offline a short while later. There was no mayday or distress signal sent out and we have not been able to pick up an emergency beacon from the Zip. And now you all know as much as I know."

"You have all been given your assignments. Heads down, asses up – get to work," she concluded.

"What's my assignment?" Zillo asked, coming up to Suki and River as they examined the map on the wall.

"We were hoping you might be able to gain access to satellites in the immediate area, see if they picked up anything," Suki replied.

"Just so we are clear," Zillo began, "You know that accessing those satellites is highly illegal?"

"Yes." Both Suki and River replied simultaneously.

Zillo grinned roguishly. "I'm on it."

Elsewhere in the condo, three students from The Academy, those with the highest marks in Suki's *Exoatmospheric Algorithms for Balancing the Effects of Visual and Auditory Instructions on Mega-Constellation Networks* class, were set up in front of dual screens, tapping away in a staccato rhythm. They were currently the brightest minds The Academy had to offer.

Suki taught the class twice a week for a hefty sum she'd negotiated shortly after being exonerated for attempted murder. River had relocated temporarily to Aurora during that time, leaving their second-in-command, Bareen, in charge, and had yet to return to Mauw for more than a visit. Suki had appointed them Office Manager at Large at *Buckles & Kwan Incorporated* for those two days she was teaching at The Academy, the Mauwian entrusted to answer phones and field incoming referrals for service. They excelled at it.

Zillo had asked for a beer shortly after his arrival and gotten such a scathing look from Suki that he had nearly turned to stone. She informed him in no uncertain terms, raising her voice to include everyone in the condo, that they would all require a clear, level head going forward and if she caught anyone consuming anything stronger than coffee, they'd have to deal with her.

And so Zillo sipped on a large mug of black bitter coffee (just the way he liked it) and kept his mouth shut. He'd set up shop in a corner on a small table and set to work. To begin, he initiated a search for whatever satellites were permanently in situ in that area and then broadened it by a few hundred miles, just to cover his bases. Once he had a comprehensive list, each gleaned from public access records, he set about bypassing each individual system, hacking not only into their current feed but the backup recordings.

This would be a piece of cake.

All he needed to do was focus on the task at hand and stop worrying about Roxy.

CHAPTER SIX

The shriek of a siren pierced the silence. Brie shot up from her chair, the words she had been speaking swallowed up by the cacophony.

"Support system failure," came the computerized voice. "Support system failure."

"The cryo-pods! Ingrid," Brie shouted to her second-in-command, "go!"

All at once there was a flurry of activity as the crew jumped to their feet and bolted from the room, following Ingrid as she led the charge; Brie was not far behind. Caught up in the chaos, the fear and confusion, Roxy ran with them, their desperate sense of urgency spurring her on. Along the winding corridors, lights flashed and the siren whooped.

Shouted exclamations from the crew were muted and incomprehensible in the pandemonium. Roxy had no idea what was going on.

Brie, having overtaken the lead, burst through a set of doors at the end of a corridor. She smashed her hand against a large green button on a panel and suddenly the siren stopped. She began to shout orders.

"Find the pods that are malfunctioning. Get them out. Now."

The crew scattered. Roxy held back, unsure how to help and not wanting to get in the way. Brie called for her.

"Roxy, help me get this open."

Muscles straining, groans could be heard around the room as two people to a pod struggled to wrench them open.

"The support system inside the pod is failing," Brie panted. "But the override on opening the seal remains. Put your back into it, Roxy."

Roxy braced her feet, clenched her teeth and pulled. An audible pop echoed from across the room; Roxy renewed her effort. The door released with a searing suction sound and Roxy stumbled backward, nearly falling. Brie leaned over and began to remove the monitors and leads from the person inside. It was a child.

"She's not breathing!" Brie yelled. "Help me get her out," she demanded.

Roxy grabbed the child's feet and together they placed her flat on the floor. Brie positioned the child's head, listened to her chest.

"I need your help. I'll do compressions, you do the breath."

They worked in tandem, no break.

"Come on, kid. Come on," Brie muttered. "Keep going," she directed at Roxy.

With a shuddering gasp, the child regained consciousness. She began to cry.

"It's okay, sweetheart, we've got you." Brie turned to Roxy. "Take care of her, her name is Victoria. I need to help get the others out."

Roxy blinked at the crying girl and had never felt more out of her depth. Roxy had never even held a baby, let alone comforted a small child. What did one do in this situation? Roxy looked around for some direction but the room had descended into chaos. She was on her own.

"Hey, uh, it's okay. You'll be alright." She patted the little girl on the shoulder. Suddenly, the child launched herself into Roxy's arms and clung to her neck. Roxy held her and stroked her hair while the child's tears soaked into her shoulder.

Across the room, life-saving measures were being administered to the occupants of four other cryopods that had failed. Roxy saw one prone figure on the ground, covered in a white sheet. Another group finally gave up in frustration, their patient beyond revival. They sat back on the floor, the very picture of defeat.

Brie caught Roxy's eye. She gestured towards the girl in Roxy's arms and then towards the doors, indicating they should leave. Roxy did not need to be told twice. She could see several crew moving to drape covers over the other casualties. She stood, the girl's arms still wrapped around her, her face buried in Roxy's neck. She ran with her from the room, skirting around the dead bodies littering the ground, trying to shield Victoria as best she could.

She had a feeling those two white sheets now

meant this little child was an orphan.

***

The child had gone to sleep on Ingrid's bed, covered in a warm blanket, her face still wet with tears. Roxy paced the room, not wanting to leave her alone in case she woke but, at the same time, longing to be a part of the action happening outside, wanting to know what was happening. A light knock came at the door and Brie peered inside.

"How is she?" Brie whispered, spotting the girl in bed.

"Cried herself to sleep." Roxy ran a hand across her face.

"Let's talk outside." Brie motioned with her hand. "Ingrid will be here to sit with her shortly. She has five younger siblings. She'll know what to do."

Roxy followed Brie through the door, closing it softly behind her. She crossed her arms, clearly angry. "You brought a child with you on a Seeker mission?"

"Her parents were a part of the program," Brie explained, her cheeks flushing. "They had no other family and refused to leave her behind to be raised in foster care. We desperately needed their expertise, so an exception was made."

"An exception?" The disapproval was evident in Roxy's voice.

"Against my better wishes," Brie admitted. "But I was overruled. I was permitted to pick my crew but the Relocation Board had final say on the passengers.

Gavin and Debra Slater were the best of the best in their field, experts in bioengineering. We needed them."

"I bet they'd regret that decision now," Roxy retorted. "Do you wish you'd fought them on it?"

Brie glanced at the door, thinking of the small girl sleeping behind it. "More than you could ever know."

CHAPTER SEVEN

Earth, 100 years ago (more or less)

"Captain Brie Nova reporting for duty, sir." Brie saluted and stood, ramrod straight, eyes straight ahead.

"At ease, Captain." Major Matthew Pascal smiled wryly at Brie. "You can forgo the formalities today."

Brie nodded, relaxed her shoulders, but maintained her rigid stance.

"I wanted to speak with you first, Captain, before I bring in the rest of the crew for the briefing. Please, take a seat."

Brie folded herself into one of the chairs placed at the front of the Major's desk. She took in the neatly arranged files on the desk, the pictures of the Major and his family: wife, two daughters, golden retriever. She felt a pang of jealousy deep in her belly and then immediately suppressed it.

Major Pascal seated himself, placed his elbows on the desk and tented his hands.

"It's not good news, I'm afraid." A dark expression passed over his face and Brie felt her heart sink.

"The Seeker?" she asked, needing confirmation of the rumors she had heard, the whispers floating around the barracks.

"Yes," he replied, somber. "The worst news imaginable, I'm afraid."

"Which one?" she managed to ask.

"*The Hawk*. We continued to track it as it left Earth's atmosphere and for a while it remained on our radar... then it dropped. We were not able to regain contact. There was no mayday, no distress signal from the ship." He frowned, the wrinkles in his forehead becoming more pronounced. "At this stage we are unsure exactly what happened up there, but it was not good."

Brie struggled to control her breathing. She would not lose control of herself in front of the Major. It was difficult but she maintained her stoic expression.

It had been their last resort. Population explosion, pollution, lack of resources, a dwindling ozone layer; all reasons why the time had come to search out alternate options.

Eight months ago, The Great Interstellar Blip had wiped out all civilian electronics and communication. The response was... predictable. Riots, looting, a world gone mad. No rule, no direction. Chaos.

It was, for the most part, back under control thanks to swift military intervention. Several anti-government factions still remained. They were monitored but otherwise left to their own devices. Then there were the so-called *Abiders*. A small group that had gained momentum as it became more and more obvious that the Earth could not continue to sustain its inhabitants in its current condition. They believed the end was nigh, and that it should be accepted, even embraced. There had already been plans to branch out beyond their own planet, but in light of recent events, the timeline had been drastically shortened. The Abiders condemned the idea vehemently.

And yet, the decision had already been made. Five Seeker ships, each sent out by The Relocation Board with two hundred souls on board each vessel, passengers and crew together, in search of hospitable planets conducive to human life. A second Earth if they were lucky enough.

Now, disaster. A lost ship, so many lost lives, so many lost opportunities. What if that had been the one ship headed in the right direction? They would never get the chance to find out.

"That brings me to why I have called you here," the Major said.

Brie jumped, having been lost in thought. Quickly she steadied herself and asked, "What do you need me to do? How can I be of service?"

"The final ship, number six, if you remember, was the one that had to remain behind for minor repairs; it's ready now. It has passed inspection and is fit to fly. Preparations have been expedited of course, we need to get this show on the road and there's no time to waste. We plan to launch in a few days. I realize that this is incredibly short notice but we would like you, Captain Nova, to helm *The Falcon*. I cannot think of anyone better suited to the job."

Brie reacted with shock. She couldn't even hide it. The significance of the four stripes sewn on her shoulder was not lost on her but she had never expected to be entrusted with a monumental task such as this.

"What do you say, Captain?" Major Pascal finally asked after the silence in the office grew.

Brie snapped her heels together, stiffened her spine. She saluted the Major and tried to keep her cool but she couldn't wipe the satisfied smile off of her face. "It would be an honor, sir."

CHAPTER EIGHT

"How far do you think you traveled?" Roxy inquired. "Before things went to shit?"

"Honestly, it's really hard to say. There was no one on board who would have been awake to monitor things." Brie squinted down at the documents spread out on the table in front of them. "Everything on *The Falcon* was controlled by someone on Earth, sort of like flying a drone. From then on, it was ferried by autopilot once we reached a certain distance outside of Earth's atmosphere. They would have made sure we were on the right trajectory and continued to track us for as long as they could, and then ground control would have flipped the switch to turn things over to the automatic systems. They are – should have been – state of the art. The data here is woefully incomplete. It shouldn't be, but it is."

"Someone fucked up," Roxy stated.

"To put it bluntly, yes," Brie replied. She pushed several sheets towards Roxy. "Have a look at this."

"It just says *unavailable* over and over."

"Correct," Brie said. "But it shouldn't. There

should be detailed information on these sheets, flight coordinates, records of any issues, etc."

"Is there a recording device on this ship?" Roxy asked. "Like a black box-type thing?"

Brie nodded. "Of course. We just don't have the energy reserves to fire it up and listen to it."

Roxy swore. "I think I smell sabotage."

"What's the plan, Captain? How are you going to get us out of this mess?"

Roxy looked up from the flight logs at the same time as Brie. A short, dark haired, heavily-built man stood in front of them with his hands on his hips. His stance was aggressive, a sour look soiled his face. Anger rolled off him in waves.

"We're working on it, Jay."

"Maybe you should work faster," Jay spat. "People are dying in case you haven't noticed."

Brie flinched. "Trust me, I am well aware of what is happening here. We are working as fast as we can."

"It's getting colder in the living quarters. There is frost on the windows. Those of us that survived the crash and the pod malfunctions... are we now going to freeze to death?" Spittle flew from his lips. "For a Captain, you seem to care very little for the people you are supposed to be in charge of. You're the leader. You're supposed to **lead**."

Roxy pushed back her chair, ready to stand. Brie placed a restraining hand on her arm.

"I understand your fear, Jay." He bristled, but she continued, "We are all in the same boat here. I do not want to lose anyone else but we need time to figure things out. This isn't a sitcom. The problem isn't going to be solved in twenty minutes."

He stared at her for a moment, teeth clenched. Then he turned on his heel and left, disappearing into the corridor beyond.

"Yikes," Roxy exclaimed. "What's with that guy?"

"He's scared," Brie replied, turning back to the logs on the table in front of her.

"He's an ass," Roxy said.

"That too," Brie agreed, laughing.

They bowed their heads together once again. By consulting the ship's auto-recorded flight logs, Roxy and Brie had hoped to narrow down their location – what they would do with this information once they had it, they weren't sure. Where the downed ship, and now the downed Zip, currently resided, was unknown. It was simply a desire for information. Nothing in this area had been mapped, of that, Roxy was positive – she would have known. She'd flown this same route many times. Her radar had never picked up on it.

"How does a whole entire planet just hide out of sight like that?" Brie wondered aloud.

"I have no idea. I have definitely heard of ghost planets, stories and such, but I always thought it was just an urban legend," Roxy offered, "like a story your parents or your siblings tell you when you're a kid to scare you." Seeing the inquisitive look on Brie's face, she continued: "Ghost planets. Basically planets that have been deemed inhospitable or were a write off for some other reason. As time goes by they tend to fade from the mind, they die off, they become *ghosts*. Cartographers stop putting them on maps because there is no reason to. They're essentially useless to those who travel through space. And they're far enough off the beaten path that there's no chance of running into them. Until now apparently."

"Well I, for one, am glad it's here," Brie mused.

"Me too," Roxy replied. "And if we play our cards right, hopefully this ghost planet doesn't end up being a god damned graveyard."

CHAPTER NINE

Sam paced the confines of his berth. Agitation rolled off of him in waves. He clenched his fists; he wanted to punch something. Or someone.

Roxy needed him.

And he was too damned far away to do anything about it. He had never been very good at expressing emotion, he had struggled, even when he had been in a relationship with Roxy, to tell her how he felt. He wished he had back then. He wished he had before he left on this mission

Right now he felt angry and useless and claustrophobic. The walls were closing in on him, he was trapped out here.

He considered the options available to him, few though they were at the moment. There was no way he would be permitted to turn the ship around and even if he physically could with a craft this large, he would never get clearance from The PRC to do so. He was stuck in a trap of his own making.

The information Suki had to share with him was minimal. He could call a few people he knew for sure, perhaps track down and pass along some classified maps; maybe even some tech that Zillo didn't even have access to. Which would be great but he wanted to be there, feet on the ground, leading the charge.

He had agreed to give Roxy space. He knew she needed it but he regretted it immensely. He loved her and if he was completely honest with himself, he had never stopped. Even when Roxy had hated him, had thought the worst of him, hadn't stood by him during his incarceration – he had understood why she felt that way. That was why he had gone on this Mission, to give her that space. He wanted her to realize it too – that she loved him and still wanted to be with him. Surely she still loved him, right?

Absence makes the heart grow fonder.

That is utter bullshit, Sam thought, *I never should have left*.

***

He couldn't get to sleep. He tossed and turned in his small bunk, an almost impossible feat given the size of the bunk and the size of him. He couldn't get Roxy off his mind, even when he dozed he dreamed of her and where she might be, who she might be with, wondering if she was hurt... or worse.

He rolled out of bed, giving up on sleep. Cursing, he hauled on the same clothes he'd worn that day, not caring what he looked like, just wanting to feel like he was doing something. He left the room, heading for the comms station, needing to do something to occupy his mind.

The room was empty. Through the porthole Sam could see they were traveling at a decent clip. He keyed in his identification and password on the small keypad attached to the wall, accessing The PRC portal. This would grant him access to a large number of classified documents and maps, anything that The Planetary Regulation Committee had amassed over the years.

He entered in the last coordinates that Suki had records of for Roxy, the last known location of the Zip, the last signal sent out before… whatever had happened. Sam couldn't even think about it.

He raked his hands through his hair, sparse though it was these days, and released a hiss of frustration though his teeth. He tried to focus on the screens in front of him.

Predictably: wide open space.

He didn't want to admit it to himself but he was scanning for any sign that the Zip might have met with disaster. He gave a sigh of relief when nothing major stood out; no space trash or flotsam, no pieces of the ship floating around out there. There were also no obstructions of note, no asteroids or anything else that could cause a catastrophic collision. At least, nothing that could take down a fully-equipped Zip with all its bells and whistles. Not with a seasoned pilot at the helm like Roxy Buckles.

Anxiety gnawed at him. His stomach was in knots. Where was Roxy?

He'd been away from her for so long. Ten hellish years in hiding, knowing that she thought he had done the unimaginable. Trying desperately to hold onto a sliver of hope that one day Roxy would know the truth, that things might even get back to the way they were before his life had fallen apart – it was what had kept him going. It was what continued to keep him going. It had been a long time since he had felt secure, had had a home and someone to care about him, to worry about him. He longed for the stability of home and family.

He shook his head to dispel the thoughts of a past long gone and a future he might never have. He had to focus on the here and now. Sam copied the screens, tapped out a hurried note, and then quickly sent the whole thing to Suki, praying it would help in some small way.

He widened the scope of his search, privy to, due to the nature of his job, the location of clandestine PRC ships otherwise cloaked to civilian observers, to undercover missions and their intel, known only to those on the craft and their handlers at The PRC.

Nothing. Still nothing.

Just wide open space.

Sam cursed loudly, the epitaph echoing around the cold, sterile room, booming back at him. He was running out of ideas.

Unless…

There was one person on this ship who might have access to even more than him, a mere PRC lackey. There would be undisclosed satellites, furtive missions still being carried out, things hidden under the darkest of covers – perhaps even more that The

PRC itself could access.

And that person was in the belly of this ship – heading straight towards a life sentence.

Sam stood, hands on his hips, tense with indecision.

He looked around the room. The very scum of Aurora was laid out peacefully below him, the cryopods strictly maintained. They were sleeping peacefully through the quiet hiss and hum of the support systems. Sam was not.

The irony was not lost on him.

Dare he try to make a deal with the devil?

He stepped up to the control panel, hesitating only for a second before tapping in his credentials. He quickly scanned the list of criminals housed on the sub-deck, seeking one ID number in particular, one he had made sure to memorize from the pre-flight manifesto.

It wasn't there.

He closed his eyes for a second. *You're just tired, that's all*, Sam thought. *That was the problem.*

He checked again.

Heart thudding, Sam opened up the main folder, scrolling through the master list of all prisoners reposing on *The Quentin*. He **must** be missing something. Chewing on his bottom lip, fast running out of other ideas, he opened a search field and typed in the full name.

He expelled a harsh breath and took a step back in shock. He couldn't believe it.

He opened a small box next to the panel, then hit

the large red button inside that was rarely, if ever, used. An ear-splitting siren whooped throughout the ship. Sam winced as it echoed within the same chamber where he stood, bouncing off the walls. Those in the cryo-pods would slumber on, blissfully unaware of the noise and the chaos; the rest of the crew on *The Quentin* would now need to be on the highest alert.

Former PRC Commander Seth Carmine was nowhere on the prison ship's list of passengers. He would have been scanned upon entry, his name added to the log, and again, when placed into his assigned cryo-pod. He **should** be on the manifest.

It all left Sam wondering, since he had been the one to march the man onto the ship himself... who had been the one to march him right back off? Who was the traitor?

And just where the hell was Carmine right now?

***

"He's not on the ship," Sam blurted as soon as the call connected, not even saying hello.

"What? Who?" Suki demanded, her voice slurred, a little disorientated after having finally dozed off. She had been awake for forty-eight hours straight.

"Carmine, dammit, that's who. He's not coded on the manifest."

"Wait," Suki was coming to her senses. "Didn't you escort—"

"I did," Sam interrupted.

"So, that means," Suki responded, "that someone else walked him right back off."

"Fuck." All of Sam's anger and frustration could be felt through that one small word.

"Does Durand know?" asked Suki, naming the current PRC Commander.

"I've got officers sweeping the ship to confirm. I have to cover all my bases. I need to be absolutely sure. Then I'll officially raise the alarm," Sam replied. "But Suki..."

"I know," Suki said, her tone grim. "He might have Roxy. We have to find her. And, Sam... **you** need to find whoever the traitor is aboard your ship."

CHAPTER TEN

Tension radiated from Suki. She motioned towards the door with her head, beckoning River. "Get Zillo. Meet me outside, in the hall," she hissed.

Suki leaned against the wall in the narrow passageway outside Roxy's condo. Times like these, she was glad that Roxy owned the entire floor and they didn't have to deal with curious neighbors. She was tired. She was cranky. Pain was radiating from hip to ankle and she leaned heavily on her cane, trying to take the pressure off. She feared she would soon need to medicate herself even though she desperately wanted to keep a clear head.

River and Zillo slipped through the door, pulling it closed behind them.

"What's wrong? Is there news?" Zillo asked eagerly.

"I just spoke with Sam." She swallowed, hard. "They can't find Carmine."

Silence followed her statement. River and Zillo stared at her, blinking.

"Did you hear me?" she finally asked.

River nodded but didn't say a word.

Finally, Zillo appeared to regain the ability to speak. He exploded: "How the fuck did that happen? Isn't Sparrow supposed to be some hotshot PRC guy now? This is on him. This is negligence. If I see him…"

River placed a paw on Zillo's shoulder. He visibly calmed.

"Zippo, my friend," River said. "You must understand that Carmine still has supporters and very likely is still, in some aspects, a very powerful man. We must not accuse Sam."

Zillo huffed and crossed his arms across his chest, not quite ready yet to absolve Sam of any blame, if he ever would. "What do we do now? What's the plan?"

Suki pushed past them, pausing with her hand on the door. "We get to work. I don't want anyone else to know. But now the real push is on."

Back inside the condo, Suki, River, and Zillo came together in a huddle in the kitchen.

"Sam sent some maps, a few scans of the area where the Zip was last seen. We will analyze these down to the very last speck of matter." Suki's voice was steel.

She grabbed everything and passed it to Lark, one of the students she'd recruited from her class at The Academy. Despite having been all "voluntold" that they would help with the cause, they were hard workers and pitched in equally and enthusiastically. Reine and Jo were watching a seemingly endless recording of all air traffic recorded on public access cameras, jotting down time stamps if anything of note popped up.

Zillo sat, his posture tense, in front of a small screen, his fingers tapping rhythmically in the air in front of him; lines of text and numbers scrolled ceaselessly across the screen.

Suki walked up behind him, her cane thumping along with her. Zillo jumped all the same when she gently called his name.

"Sorry, didn't mean to frighten you," Suki apologized.

"Hey, no worries," he replied, barely glancing up from what he was doing.

"Maybe you should take a break?" Suki suggested. "You're going to give yourself bad posture hunched over like that. There are some PWR Protein Delite™ bars the kids brought with them."

"No time," he replied in clipped tones, "I'm close."

Suki was afraid to ask *close to what?* Hearing the news of Carmine's escape, or whatever had happened, Zillo had shut himself away in a corner, ignoring everyone else, not eating, drinking only the strongest coffee he could find in Roxy's meager cupboard.

"Perhaps you would care to share with the rest of us what it is that you are doing, Zero," River cajoled. They had approached quietly while Suki and Zillo spoke. Neither of them ever corrected River, it was pointless – they never got Zillo's name right and it was easier to just let it slip past and carry on.

Zillo finally stopped, reluctantly, and turned to face both Suki and River. He licked his lips, strangely unsure of himself. Suki even thought he looked a little nervous.

"I'm hacking The PRC mainframe," he admitted reluctantly, sotto voce.

Suki's eyes widened. "That's impossible."

"Is it though?" Zillo asked and beckoned them closer. "I'm almost in. I can access cameras, drones, and security footage from PRC ships, both past and present. If I get in, we'll have even more intel than Sparrow can give us."

Suki and River exchanged a glance.

"Alexzander," Suki began. It was the first time she had ever used his full name. "You could be sanctioned for this. It will be considered an act of treason."

Zillo scoffed. "You didn't seem so concerned with illegal hacking earlier. Besides, the only person committing treason here is Carmine. And I'm going to find him. We're getting Roxy back, Suki, if it's the last thing I do." He turned back to his work, his cheeks flushed, his jaw clenched.

Suki nodded slowly, knowing Zillo didn't expect a response. She took River's elbow and led them away, back to the safety of the kitchen.

"I believe he may be…" Suki trailed off, looking back at Zillo, his face set in determination as he continued to tap aggressively in the air.

"It is an undeniable fact, my dear Suki," River said softly. "That man is in love with Roxy Buckles."

"Well, crap," Suki responded. "As if we needed things to be any more fucking complicated."

***

The crew had searched the entire ship. It had taken an abhorrent amount of time but Sam was insistent that they be thorough. There was no sign of disgraced former Commander Seth Carmine anywhere on the craft. With no other option on the horizon, Sam, reluctantly, made the transmission to his contact at The PRC to officially raise the alarm.

He was immediately patched through to Hadrien Durand; the conversation was brief.

Sam relayed what little information he had, then, against Suki's wishes, Sam informed Durand that Roxy was missing and unaccounted for. Durand's response was as expected. Sam knew that Durand respected and admired Roxy – he had welcomed her with open arms to The PRC. Despite Suki's insistence that they keep things on the downlow, Sam felt certain that Durand would have their back.

"Just one more thing, Commander, if I may be so bold," Sam interjected apprehensively as the call was coming to a close. This was going to be a big ask.

"Anything, Sam," Durand replied. "What can I do to help?"

Sam cleared his throat, stalling, knowing that what he was about to ask for would be near impossible. Still, he had to try.

"I have to find Roxy," Sam confessed as the silence became unbearable. "**Need** to be there. If there are any strings you can pull, any people you know who might be able to help... I want to get back to Aurora and lead the search. And I hope to make it happen as soon as possible."

***

A knock came at the door of the condo. Everyone stopped what they were doing, their senses on high alert. They looked at each other, assessing the situation and quickly realizing the potential that this scene could get real bad, real fast – depending on who was at the door. Whoever it was had been able to bypass security at the front very easily, if they were right outside the condo.

They were all here. No one else knew what was going on. For good reason, Suki had kept the group small and tight. So, who the hell was it?

With trepidation, Suki nodded at River to open the door. She saw the muscles ripple below the Mauwian's fur. River expected trouble but they were ready to pounce if the circumstances called for it.

The door opened a crack, River peeked through and then they stepped back to widen the gap, to admit their guest.

Standing at the threshold, to everyone's shock, was none other than the Commander of The PRC, security team in tow.

"Good afternoon." Hadrien Durand smiled benevolently. "I hear we have a bounty hunter to find."

***

Suki was livid.

She held it together at first, then didn't. Finally, River dragged her into Roxy's bedroom – with difficulty – and Suki really let loose.

"I am going to kill Sam Sparrow. I am going to make it slow and painful and I am going to enjoy every single moment of it."

River attempted to calm her. It was unsuccessful.

"I distinctly remember," Suki continued, pacing the room, "telling that stupid, stupid man to keep his big, fat mouth shut."

"He thought he was helping," River offered.

Suki kept going as though she hadn't heard a word. "That prick. He doesn't think we are capable of finding Roxy without him. *Oh, poor Suki, she won't be able to do it without me,*" she mocked. "He's unbearable!"

She threw her hands up and collapsed onto Roxy's bed. "What are they doing out there?"

Her anger could not quell her curiosity – she needed to know.

River peeked through a small opening in the door. "Mr. Commander is currently speaking with Zippo. It appears civil but intense."

"I'm going out there." Suki made to get up from the bed.

River rushed forward. "You must calm yourself first, Suki dear. We don't want to anger the security team." They paused. "Again."

Suki sighed. "Fine. Okay. Whatever. I'll behave."

River's tail flicked once, twice.

"I promise!" Suki insisted and, together, they exited the room.

"What do you think, can it be done?" Durand was asking Zillo as Suki and River approached the two.

"It's possible, yes," Zillo replied slowly, drawing out the words. "We have the tech, or at least the bare bones of it. It would mean rushing things, launching sooner than I would like and certainly sooner than I anticipated. There are still a few bugs to work out, some aesthetic aspects I'd like to work on."

"But you do think that it will work?" Durand asked again, then sensing some reluctance, "And if you're willing of course."

Zillo rubbed a hand across his face, scratching at the five o'clock shadow that darkened his face.

He's stalling, Suki thought.

Finally, Zillo released a small breath and replied, "I'll do my best."

Durand clapped him on the shoulder. "Good man. I knew I could count on you."

Zillo shook his head. "I'll have to go to my labs. What needs to be done cannot be done here. I won't make any promises, not until I have had a chance to check things over. I will have to be one hundred percent confident in its abilities before I consent."

Suki knew that Zillo would be reluctant to leave. He'd been here since the start and would want to see it through. She sensed his frustration but also his hesitation to say no to the Commander.

"My team will escort you," Durand offered. "It will

be much quicker. We'll get you there in no time."

Zillo nodded as Durand walked away to consult with his crew.

"What's going on?" Suki demanded in a low voice. "What does he want you to do?"

Zillo looked at her, glanced at River and then back to Suki again.

He lowered his voice and leaned in. "Durand wants my tech. CommsLink has been working on something new, something big. It could change things immensely once it's ready for release." Zillo paused.

"And?" Suki prompted.

"And," Zillo finally replied," he wants me to use it… to get Sparrow back to Aurora."

CHAPTER ELEVEN

Suki and River gaped at him.

"That's just not possible," Suki said. "*The Quentin* has passed the point of no return, he's stuck on that ship. We'd never get there in time nor would he ever get back in time. It would be months! That's not how it works. You can't do that."

Zillo was shaking his head.

"What?" Suki demanded. She was getting tired of being out of the loop.

"I can. Or I should be able to anyway. CommsLink has been making some big strides in new travel technology. We have been working on a way to compress time and space; working on a way to get to places, and back, a whole hell of a lot quicker than we presently can."

"You're kidding," Suki scoffed. "Like teleportation or something? I know you're a genius and all but that's pure fiction."

"Not quite," Zillo replied, smiling ruefully. "It's more like adding a boost, a little push to what we currently have. We can cut travel time by as much as three quarters, maybe more once I have the time to work on it. As I am sure you heard, there are a few bugs to flush out but I think I can make it happen."

"Do you want to make it happen?" River asked, getting to the heart of the matter.

Zillo looked away, his gaze lingering on the view from the condo windows. "If Sparrow thinks he can find Roxy by being back on Aurora, if he thinks he can bring her home safely, then I have no choice. I have to be on board with this. I have to make it happen." He nodded at Suki and River and turned to leave with Durand and his team.

"Keep us updated," Suki called. "Please."

He glanced over his shoulder. "Wouldn't dream of doing otherwise."

Then he was gone.

"This will be… interesting," River purred.

Suki sighed deeply. "No, my feline friend, this is going to be a complete shitshow."

***

"Hello, Sparrow."

The voice on the comm was not the one Sam had expected to hear.

"Zillinger." His tone was clipped.

"As I am sure you have been made aware, we are about six hours out from launch." Zillo was brusque, struggling to be polite. "You will need to slow your ship to the lowest speed allowable while still maintaining lift. This must be done as soon as you are given the signal."

"Got it," came Sam's curt reply.

"Look, Sparrow, let's just get this out of the way, shall we?" Zillo was deathly calm. "You don't like me, and if I'm completely honest, I don't really like you either. You're likely the whole reason we're in this mess."

Sam bristled at the implication but kept his mouth shut.

"We aren't ever going to be friends," Zillo said adamantly. "But as much as I'd prefer to leave you exactly where you are for the foreseeable future, Durand has asked this favor of me and I am doing my best to comply."

Sam laughed mockingly. "Oh, I am sure you're getting something out of this. A contract with The PRC. A payout. A favor."

"The only thing I'm getting out of this," Zillo responded, "is one extra person who wants to find Roxy just as much as the rest of us do. That's all that matters right now. Getting her home safe."

Sam was quiet for a few seconds. "Fine. Tell me what I have to do," he said, stiffly.

The men discussed the details of the changeover. The conversation was, at best, civil.

"And then, once you're back on Aurora, you can join the search," Zillo concluded. "That's if we haven't found her before then." He couldn't help the dig.

Sam bristled. "Roxy doesn't go for the hero, Zillinger. You should know that by now."

Zillo gave a short bark of laughter. "If that's the case then, fly boy, why are you in such a god damned rush to get back here and be one?"

CHAPTER TWELVE

"We'll need to wake them up." Roxy glanced at Brie. "It's a last resort, I know, but it's the only way. The pods are chewing up too much of the energy reserves."

"But, it will take time…" Brie replied.

"Which is something we have short supply of," Roxy finished.

"It must be a gradual process," Brie said. "To wake them up quickly, it won't work. That would be a death sentence. We risk seizure, a cardiac event, brain bleeds. Instant death."

"How long?" Roxy asked.

"If everyone helps… Ingrid can pitch in. We would need to divide into groups, some to monitor vitals, some to physically open the pods, some to assess those who are waking. Perhaps, close to a week?" Brie said.

"That's too long."

Brie winced. Roxy knew she was being harsh, hated to be that way, but she needed Brie to realize the gravity of the situation in front of them.

"I'm sorry, Brie. So very sorry, but we need more power or else we're going to freeze to death before there's even a chance of rescue. We cannot keep this ship humming along as it is. We might even be able to preserve enough power to try and send out a signal. Otherwise, we're **all** doomed."

Brie dropped her head into her hands. She knew it was a lose-lose situation but they didn't have any other choice.

"We'll start in the morning. I'll speak with Ingrid and then we'll let everyone know."

***

Brie had gathered the flight crew, few though they were, and the passengers who had already awoken from their pods, those who were physically capable of helping. They gathered in the cryo-pod chamber. Many of them were notably upset, some trembling, others swiping tears from their eyes.

Together, Brie and Ingrid took turns briefing those assembled on the precautions they needed to take, instructions on how to deactivate the cryo-state and how to slowly bring the person enclosed within the pod back to consciousness. They were lucky in a way – many of them had medical backgrounds or some other formal therapeutic training. Otherwise they were, in general, the best of the best in their respective fields; they were intelligent and quick to learn.

With the briefest of nods, Brie concluded her instructions.

They began.

***

It was a grueling process. Sweat dripped off the tip of Roxy's nose; she'd been assigned to help with the physically demanding task of opening the decompressed pods. The work was difficult and, at times, defeating.

They forged on for hours. The passengers who had come around, whose vitals were well, had been transported to triage rooms for further assessment and monitoring with Ingrid. She reported back that there were frightfully few of them who would make it.

Those who hadn't come out of the pods alive… They'd chosen to seal those unfortunate souls back into their pods.

Brie was relentless. She shouted orders when it was needed or, likewise, encouragement to keep going. She helped to open the pods, she pulled countless unresponsive passengers out of the pods and began life-saving measures before the lucky ones were moved to triage. She cried when one was lost. Roxy could tell that Brie's energy was ebbing away. They had no food of substance, merely a sweetened nutrient solution. It was making them weaker as time went by.

Finally, when everyone had gone well beyond their limits, Brie gave the call to stop, sliding to the floor, resting her head in her hands.

They'd only been able to save eleven.

Every single other passenger from *The Falcon* was dead.

***

There were twenty-six of them in total now including Roxy. They'd scavenged as much spare clothing as possible, bundling up against the stark cold now permeating the ship.

"It shouldn't be this cold," Roxy remarked, rubbing her hands together. "Cold, yes, but not quite this cold. It must be well below freezing here at the moment."

Brie tried unsuccessfully to suppress a shiver. "Well, I am a little out of my league, I'm afraid. I've never crash-landed on a ghost planet one hundred years in the future before."

Roxy couldn't help the laugh that escaped her. Then: "Sorry, Brie. If I don't laugh, I might cry."

"I think you might be right, Roxy," Brie relented. She sat up straighter on her chair. "Do you feel that?"

"Feel what? My ass about ready to freeze off?" Roxy retorted.

"Well that too. But… Do you feel a draft?" Brie asked.

Now Roxy sat up. She leaned forward, stretching out a cold hand, testing the air.

A cool draft caressed her already chilled skin. "What the hell?"

In unison, they jumped to their feet, trying to sense where it was coming from. They walked along the corridors, hands held out in front of them like divining rods.

"We've checked everywhere," Brie lamented

when they came up short.

"Maybe." Roxy was thinking. "There has to be somewhere that we haven't checked. Just think. There has to be one room, one area that we haven't been in. It might be a storage area or a supply closet or a–"

"Wait," Brie interrupted. "There's a small room; it's basically full of wires and harddrives that **should** have been collecting data during the trip but obviously didn't. No one goes in there. No one would have any reason to. We wouldn't need what's in there – what would have been in there – until we eventually landed."

With Brie in the lead, the two traversed the dying ship, finally stopping when they reached the dark metal bulkhead. A small trap door swung loosely on its hinges.

"This should not be open," Brie said, walking closer to take a look.

Roxy grabbed her arm, held her back. "Be careful."

Brie squeezed Roxy's hand to reassure her then stepped closer, tentatively clasping the door. She pulled her hand back quickly. "Ouch. It's freezing," she reported.

She inched forward, shouldered the trap door out of the way and in one fluid motion stuck her head in through. The sound of elaborate cursing echoed in the small chamber. Some of the words Brie was using, Roxy had never even heard before.

"What's happening?" she shouted, intrigued not only by the empty space but also the foreign-to-her expressions. She leaned closer to the headless body.

Brie was rigid with anger, still partially hanging inside the trap door opening.

Roxy backed up as Brie eased herself out. Her face was flushed despite the cold or, perhaps, because of it.

"Someone has cleaved a small fissure into the hull. It's not a huge opening by any means, not substantial enough to cause decompression or an immediate disaster. But it's sizable enough to let in the cold air." She chewed on her bottom lip as she considered a possible solution to the problem that currently presented itself. "I don't know if we have the proper materials to repair it."

"For now, let's just block up this door, seal it off and hope for the best," Roxy suggested in lieu of any other quick fix option.

"Okay, that's a start," Brie agreed. "And then I'm going to hunt down whoever did this and I am going to kick their ass."

"Atta girl," Roxy replied.

***

They did the best with what they had. Something called duct tape that Roxy had never heard of before and a thick plastic sheet. They sealed off the entrance to the hatch, for what little good it did. The cold had already permeated the ship and with no means of clearing it out or heating things back up, it would stay that way.

Back in Brie's quarters, huddled together beneath a blanket for warmth, their hands like ice, the two women mulled over this latest development.

"Any ideas?" Roxy asked. "Is there anyone on board that you would suspect of doing this?"

"I've been thinking it over," Brie confessed. "I wouldn't have said it was possible even a few days ago, definitely not when we took off from Earth. But now I am really beginning to wonder. Maybe there's a possibility we have an Abider on board."

"A what?" Roxy was perplexed. "What's an Abider?"

Brie sighed and shook her head. "There was this group of people, they were gaining momentum long before the Seeker ships were sent out. They felt that we had made a mess of things on Earth so we should just *abide* by it. They thought we should just stay where we were; they disapproved of space travel. They were getting more and more frenetic the closer we came to leaving. There were a few cases of minor vandalism, lots of protests and things like that. Maybe we inadvertently took one with us, a spy."

"Are they dangerous?" Roxy asked. "No, wait, obviously they are given the current situation."

"I wouldn't have thought so, at least, not before everything that's happened." She gestured around her. "But if they didn't mean to do harm to us, then why make that hole? Why let in the sub-freezing air?"

A sudden thought occurred to Roxy. "What if this wasn't the only thing they did, Brie?" she said in a rush. "What about the missing data, the lack of tracking?"

"Christ," Brie exclaimed, sitting up, suddenly

even more alarmed than before. "Roxy, what if this wasn't an accident at all? What if the Abiders are the reason this ship crashed here? What if they tried to kill us all from the start?"

***

It was a fitful night's sleep. The women huddled together, back to back, in the same bed to conserve heat and now, perhaps, even for safety. If there had been room enough between, they would have tossed and turned. Instead, they lay there until finally weariness overcame them.

Roxy was awake long before Brie, having only dozed off and on. Brie was snoring softly. Roxy lay still and quiet, letting the captain get as much rest as possible. They'd moved little during the night but somehow Roxy had shifted and was facing Brie. She studied her bunk mate's face, the long lashes and the smattering of freckles across the bridge of her nose and along the apple of her cheeks. A lock of hair had fallen across Brie's forehead and Roxy reached out to push it back out of her eyes, catching herself at the last minute, not wanting to wake Brie. Despite the situation that had brought her here, despite the rocky road they faced, Roxy felt strangely content lying here next to this woman, her new friend.

Brie's eyes fluttered open.

"Good morning," Roxy greeted her.

"How can you be so cheerful?" Brie asked. "It's freezing."

"I can think of worse ways to wake up," Roxy replied, smiling. "We should get back to–"

"Wait," Brie said. "Let's just talk about normal things for just a few minutes. Pretend we are anywhere but here. I'm not ready to face reality yet."

"Alright," Roxy agreed. "We can do that."

"Do you have anyone special waiting for you at home, Roxy?" Brie asked, pink suffusing her cheeks.

"I am sure I have one seriously pissed off friend-slash-business partner on a rampage right now, trying to track me down." Seeing the question on Brie's face, Roxy explained: "Suki is my best friend and also my business partner. She's... feisty. We've been through a lot together. I am sure she's frantic right now."

"Are you two..." Brie left the question open-ended.

"No, no, not like that," Roxy explained, her voice tinged with laughter. "She's basically my sister and I love her to death, just not that way. There **was** a guy. I thought maybe something might... but it wasn't the right time."

"What happened?" Brie asked sympathetically.

"My ex, Sam, showed up on the scene. There's a lot of history there. We have a past. Things we never really had a chance to resolve. And he gets me. This new guy, Zillo, he's great. He's smart, funny and kind. I didn't want him to think he was a rebound or my second choice, you know? I needed some time for myself to figure things out."

"I get it," Brie responded. "Just remember, Roxy, sometimes it's better to look to the future rather than always looking over your shoulder back into the past.

It's in the past for a reason."

Roxy nodded, considering the advice. "That makes sense. What about you? Anyone special?" she added in a rush.

Brie shook her head. "No. There was someone... We ended things shortly before I left. She said I spent too much time at work. And to be fair, she was probably right. We thought moving in together would help things but, ultimately, it made it worse. My absence was simply more noticeable with her there all the time, by herself at that. She packed up and left one day while I was at work and that was it. She didn't even leave a note."

"I'm sorry," Roxy said, reaching for Brie's hand. "That must have been very difficult."

"It made the decision to leave on this mission all the more easier." Brie smiled halfheartedly, rising from the bunk. "We should check and see how everyone is doing I guess."

Reluctantly, Roxy unfolded herself from the bed and perched on the side, blowing hot air from her mouth onto her cold hands.

"Today," Brie told her, "come hell or high water, we find out who has been sabotaging *The Falcon*."

"What's the plan?" Roxy asked.

Brie smiled, shrugged one shoulder. "I haven't quite figured that out yet but when I do..."

Roxy stood up beside her. "Whatever it is, I've got your back. One hundred percent."

CHAPTER THIRTEEN

Concealed within the vent atop The PRC Plaza, he kept silent and still, waiting until he was sure that the coast was clear. Even then, he'd waited a little while longer. There were no means of communication on him – he didn't want to be tracked and, if anyone knew that was possible, it was him who was privy to all the tricks of the trade. Especially the dirty tricks.

He removed the titanium grate quietly, slithering out from within the enclosure. He kept low to the ground, glancing furtively around into the darkness. He breathed deeply of the night air and grinned. It smelled like freedom.

Money could buy a lot of things; enough money and you could guarantee someone's silence. With the right number of extra zeros put into the right set of hands, well, you could get most anything you wanted.

Using the pilfered credentials he'd concealed within his pocket, he unlocked the door that led from the launch pad on the roof, gaining access to the top floor of the building. Creeping down the steps, avoiding the elevators, keeping to the darkest of corridors, Carmine finally reached the bottom floor. He shucked himself of the prison garb he had been wearing, revealing basic civilian clothing beneath. Nothing that would stand out; he was head to toe, drab and dull. There was a hat tossed carelessly (but for a purpose) in the corner; Carmine bent, grabbed it, and jammed it on top of his shorn locks. They'd shaved his head once he had been apprehended. He missed his hair.

Sweat beaded his brow, soaked now into the rim of the hat – he was close.

He eased the door open, made eye contact with the guard on the front door. Carmine saw the guard glance around, inside and outside, and then nod, briefly, at Carmine.

That was the signal? he thought. Somehow he'd expected something more exciting.

Carmine stepped through the door and strode purposefully across the main lobby, his head low. He winked at the guard as he breezed past him and out through the front door. The guard smirked.

He didn't pause but hit the ground running. The security cameras, should anyone care to ever check them, would have mysteriously malfunctioned at just the right time. At the end of the parking lot an off-duty *SkyShaw* driver, otherwise known as a *Roamer*, would be waiting for him, having been paid generously for their discretion.

He was in the clear.

In a few short hours, he would not only be leaving New Cosmos behind him, but Aurora as well.

Time to get the hell out of dodge, he thought to himself. *And good riddance to it.*

When, and if, he ever came back to this godforsaken planet, those assholes who did this to him... there would be absolute hell to pay.

CHAPTER FOURTEEN

"Have any of you heard from Zillo?" Suki threw out into the room, raising her voice to be heard above the busy sounds of people hard at work: tapping, the rustling of papers, the low murmur of conversation.

River stopped what they were doing (scanning even more charts and maps) to answer. "There has been no change since you asked that question ten minutes ago, Suki dear."

Suki cursed under her breath. It felt longer than that. Zillo had been gone for twenty-four hours without contact. She leaned against the table, rubbing her palms against her eyes; they felt gritty and sore. She couldn't remember the last time she had slept more than a few minutes at a time, cat naps snatched while sitting up, in between bouts of analyzing CoCo printouts as more information flowed in.

Suki did not enjoy this feeling. She felt untethered. Like she was floating in space, waiting for – hoping for – someone or something to grab her and pull her back down to Aurora.

She still had no idea where Roxy was. Or if she

was even alive. No, she couldn't think that way. She had to be alive. There was no other option. But as hard as she tried, the terrifying thought kept creeping back into Suki's brain, burrowing, like a parasite looking for a host.

Roxy was alive... wasn't she?

A loud buzz and CoCo changed her display to an incoming transmission.

It was Zillo.

A large projection of his face filled the wall.

Suki moved closer, in range of CoCo's eye so that Zillo could see her as well.

"Zillo?" Suki needed to say no more, he knew what she was asking.

He nodded his head. "I think I've got something."

"Is it Carmine?"

"No," he replied, "something better."

***

Zillo sent a personal *SkyShaw* to collect Suki and River. The three Academy students were sent on their way, Suki telling them they'd be exempt from their final paper for their contributions to the search. They could be heard whooping for joy as they headed down the hall.

Suki tapped her fingers impatiently against her cane as the *SkyShaw* lifted off from outside the condo and into the ever-present city lights of New Cosmos. Beside her, River Lynx was the living picture of serenity. *How can they be so calm?* Suki wondered and then gave voice to her thoughts.

"How can you be so calm about this?"

"It is the Mauwian way," River responded cryptically.

"Okay," Suki drawled out. "What does that even mean?"

"I do not know, Suki dear. It is what I have always been told. The queen who birthed me and my siblings taught us to be still and thoughtful in the face of adversity, to think before we respond, to assess the world around us and then act accordingly."

"Alright," Suki responded thoughtfully. "And what would the queen tell you you should do once you do all that, if there is still a threat?"

"Claw their eyes out," River replied, chuckling, their sharp little front teeth flashing white in the glow of the interior.

The *SkyShaw* arrived shortly in front of CommsLink, touching down gently before the doors hissed open to permit their exit. This particular one was automated; there had been no need for conversation or negotiation of payment. Suki and River stepped out and the *SkyShaw* immediately flew away in the direction of the back of the building.

"Have you ever been here before?" River asked, looking around skeptically.

"Roxy says it's bigger on the inside," Suki replied.

"Someone has said this to me before," River mused. "A funny man with a spatula..."

"A spatula?" Suki asked, her nose wrinkled in

confusion. It was hard to follow River sometimes.

River rubbed a paw across their chin thoughtfully. "Perhaps it was a screwdriver."

"We should go inside."

"Yes, let's do that. And see what Zero has to tell us."

The interior lights were dim, there was no one at the front reception desk. Suki and River entered cautiously.

"Hello," Suki called out, wary.

There was no response. Then a soft ding as a set of doors opened across the foyer, one of several along a bank of elevators.

"Shall we?" River asked.

They headed for the open door and stepped through. By the time they had turned around, the elevator was already moving.

"Are we going up or down?" Suki wondered aloud.

"I believe… up." River replied, sniffing at the air.

After a short trip, the elevator dinged again and the doors whooshed open.

"Welcome!" It was Zillo.

"Man, you look like shit." Suki heard River gasp beside her. "What? It's true."

Zillo chucked. "It's okay, River, I am well aware of what I look like at the moment. I've taken breaks to shower but that's about it."

His thick dark hair stuck up in unruly tufts all over his head. Several days of growth covered his face, dark circles shadowed beneath his eyes. His shirt sleeves were rolled up to his elbows, there was a smudge of something that might have been grease streaked across his forehead. He still, somehow, managed to remain ruggedly handsome.

"Follow me."

River and Suki trailed along with Zillo down a long hall with doors on either side. All were closed. Zillo paused at the end of the hall.

"This is my office." He pushed the door open and beckoned them inside.

It wasn't what Suki was expecting. It was sparsely furnished. A large antique desk, likely from the late 2020's took up most of the space. Two comfortable-looking chairs sat in front of it. That was it. No paintings or digital prints, no objets d'art.

Zillo seemed to sense what she was thinking. He shrugged apologetically. "I don't actually spend much time in this room. You're more likely to find me in the underground labs. Have a seat, please. I have something to show you."

His excitement was contagious. Suki leaned forward in the chair.

"I'm sorry." He stopped abruptly. "I'm a terrible host. Would either of you like a drink? Or a snack? Coffee or water? Protein smoothie?"

"Zillo," Suki began, her voice deathly calm. "If you don't hurry up and tell me what you have found, I will be forced to hurt you."

"I am with Suki on this one," River agreed. "I will have to bring out the claws."

Zillo started to laugh, then sobered at the look on their faces. "Right-oh."

He pressed a button on his desk and a large monitor materialized from the wall behind.

"I found a brief mention of it in an archived file, ported over from old Earth files. Once I had that, I was able to work my way backwards. It wasn't easy. Half this stuff is still on paper, back on Earth. I have a contact though and he got me this."

"What am I looking at here?" Suki asked, squinting.

"You're looking at the solar system, circa 2005."

"Damn," Suki breathed. "It's so... small." She stood and walked closer for a better look. "It's also super weird seeing a round sun."

"I mapped the coordinates of Roxy's last known location using this map and some pretty ancient technology. I called in a few favors. And this," he gestured to a section of the screen, "right here is where they lead."

"There's nothing there," Suki said, her frustration quite apparent. "This isn't new information, Zillo. We've known this for ages."

"Look a little closer, Suki."

Suki squinted her eyes, moving closer. "Come on, man, can you zoom in or something? Help me out here."

Zillo sighed dramatically but did as she requested. "See it now?" he asked.

Her head swiveled around towards him. "Is that...?

"Sure is," Zillo replied.

Suki let out a low whistle. "Well holy shit."

CHAPTER FIFTEEN

Brie handed their asses to them on a silver platter. She paced in front of the assembled group, rhyming off their indiscretions, and exactly what punishment she would meter out when she found the culprit.

For once Roxy was happy to take a backseat, to let someone else lead the charge. She understood now how Brie had reached the rank of Captain: she was glorious.

Even Jay, the burly guy who had often disparaged Brie for their current situation, flinched in the face of her fury.

"If the person responsible for this act of terrorism would care to turn themselves in now, it would save me the trouble of hunting you down," Brie spat, pacing in front of the crowd. "Vandalism of a government ship, murder, attempted murder – I will have your head."

"How do you know it ain't her?" Jay sneered, pointing at Roxy.

"Because, Jay," Brie began, rubbing her head slowly, "Roxy wasn't on Earth a hundred years ago so she could not have sabotaged the ship."

A few passengers snickered. Jay crossed his arms and sulked.

"Please, if you have information, even something small or seemingly insignificant, share it. Tell me, or if you don't want to come to me, Ingrid will listen to what you have to say without judgment."

"I am here if anyone needs to talk," Ingrid added, briefly patting Brie's arm in solidarity.

The ragtag group in front of them, bundled in an assortment of mismatched clothing to keep warm, shuffled off, breaking into smaller cliques, murmuring amongst themselves.

"I will go and see if I can find some more blankets," Ingrid told them, smiling.

"Thank you, Ingrid, that would be helpful," Brie replied.

Ingrid turned to the small child next to her. "Victoria, would you like to help me?"

The little girl nodded and the two went off together.

Roxy put her hand on Brie's shoulder encouragingly. "That was great. I think you got through to them; hopefully now they realize just how dire the situation is."

"Yeah, for what good it did." She sighed and slid to the floor in the passageway, her head in her hands. "We're still back to square one. What do we do now?"

Brie took a shuddering breath. Roxy slid down beside her, putting an arm around her shoulders.

"Brie, as difficult as it is…" Roxy paused. "What we talked about… it might be our only option. Using the backup energy sources to send out one last Hail Mary SOS. It might be our only chance."

"That won't leave us with much power, if any. We won't survive for long after that."

Roxy nodded. "I know. But at least we can say we tried. If we don't, we all die anyway."

Brie's shoulders dropped. She was exhausted.

"You should get some rest. Today has been a lot."

Roxy stood up and helped Brie to her feet. They shuffled together side by side down the hall, lights dulling and flickering as they traversed the passageway that would lead them to their sleeping quarters.

Roxy wondered how long they would have before the lights went out for good.

***

They very nearly made it.

Rounding the corner, at the joint where the main hall joined the berth section, they found their way through blocked by a small gathering of passengers who'd formed a barrier. His arms folded across his expansive chest, Jay stood at the front of the group – he was clearly the leader.

This wasn't a coincidence, this was a confrontation.

"We're cold, we're tired, and we're hungry. You're doing nothing to help us," Jay snapped, his fiery gaze locked on Brie. The five or so standing behind him nodded their agreement. "All you're doing is trying to put the blame on us."

"That's ridiculous, Jay, and you know it," Brie retorted. "We are doing everything we can to get everyone off of this ship, safe and sound. You knew the risks when you applied to be a part of it."

"No one expected this to happen," he scoffed.

"Perhaps not," Brie replied. "But you signed the contract, you accepted the risks, and it was always a possibility, no matter how small we expected that possibility would be."

"This is your fault, Captain Nova. Our friends are dead because of **you**." Jay didn't even raise his voice but the words echoed in the chamber with as much force as if he had.

Brie gasped. A few of the faces behind Jay appeared surprised at the accusation, at the direction this was taking.

Roxy stepped forward. "Enough. How can you all stand there, presumably a bunch of very educated people, and accuse the one person who is doing everything in their power to save you? Blame her for things that were out of her control? She wasn't piloting this ship. She didn't bring it down. It wasn't pilot error. If anything—"

"No," Brie interrupted.

"Brie," Roxy responded. "You can't keep this quiet."

"What the hell are you talking about?" Jay demanded.

"Someone **purposefully** caused the crash of *The Falcon*. Someone aboard this ship has been sabotaging your mission long before now and they are continuing to do so. It's not your Captain that you need to blame here, it's the person who put you in this position in the first place," Roxy concluded, breathing hard.

"You're full of shit," Jay retorted, but he didn't seem so sure of himself anymore.

Roxy braced herself. She knew, when people started to feel that way, especially people like Jay, things usually got a little dirty.

That was okay. Sometimes Roxy liked getting dirty. She saw his jaw clench right before he took a step forward. Brie placed a restraining hand on Roxy's arm.

"Jay," Brie said in a warning, "relax."

But he was too far gone now. Full of fear and anger and hubris, he knew no other way to express it except by lashing out.

Perhaps it wasn't the time nor the place, Roxy acknowledged, but then she grinned and put up her hands, urging him on. "Come on, big fella, show me what you got."

"I can't hit a civilian, especially a lady," Jay scoffed.

"Lucky for you," Roxy retorted. "'Cause I sure as hell ain't no lady."

"I have a black belt." Jay placed his hands on his hips.

Roxy rolled her eyes. "I don't know what that is, but good for you. Seems to me you're just scared you're going to get beat up by a girl."

Jay's face flushed. Without warning, he rushed towards Roxy, low and quick. She was ready for him. She used his own momentum against him; sidestepping the hit, she dropped and swung a leg, connecting with the back of his knee. He went down like a felled tree.

Winded from the fall, he jumped to his feet and approached Roxy with his fists up. "Bitch," he muttered.

"You don't even know the half of it." Roxy laughed. "How about this," she offered generously, "I'll let you have one free punch before I kick your ass up into your mouth."

"Roxy, be careful," Brie warned.

"Always am," Roxy replied, grinning, feeling like herself more than she had for days. She'd been so stationary since crash-landing the Zip. Despite the bruises and the sore muscles from the crash, she needed to stretch and move, and what better way to get the kinks out than a good, old-fashioned fight.

His fist shot out, connecting with Roxy's face, splitting her lip. Jay looked pleased with himself. Roxy turned her head and spat blood onto the floor.

"That all you got?" she asked, facing him. The smirk fell off his face.

"I'm going to knock you the fuck–" Jay didn't get to finish his sentence. Roxy rushed him, taking him by surprise. The two crashed to the floor, rolling. Roxy twisted herself on top, pinning Jay's arms above his head, weighing him down. He struggled to no avail, finally going limp beneath her.

Breathing heavily, he looked up at Roxy. "You know," he murmured, licking his lips. "Under different circumstances, this would be pretty hot."

Roxy glared at him for a second, then head-butted him in the nose. Blood trickled from his nostrils and down the sides of his face. He wasn't aware of it though.

"Guess I knocked **you** the fuck out," Roxy replied, getting to her feet. "Anyone else?" she asked, addressing Jay's gang.

They quickly retreated.

"Roxy, you're bleeding," Brie lamented.

"I'm fine," Roxy replied, swiping a hand across her mouth. "This is nothing, trust me."

"You didn't have to do that, you know."

Roxy couldn't help but laugh. "I know. I feel a lot better now though, I must admit. He needed to be put in his place." Then, sobering, she quickly asked, "Do you think **he's** the Abider? He's certainly enough of a dickhole to be the one doing all of this."

Brie looked down at the prone figure on the ground. "How can someone so smart be **this** dumb?" she asked.

"Book smarts don't always mean common sense," Roxy replied. "Should we tie him up?"

"Nah, just leave him." Brie kicked at Jay's foot. He was still out cold. "He'll be scared shitless of you now. I don't think he'll give us much trouble."

CHAPTER SIXTEEN

Sam was rattled. He hated waiting.

He paced back and forth along the access hall, grinding his teeth, running over and over in his mind what he planned to do once he set foot back on Aurora. He counted them off in his head:

1. Find Roxy
2. Find Carmine
3. Smash Carmine's face
4. Find the traitor aboard *The Quentin*
5. Convince Roxy that they belonged together

His wristlet buzzed.

"Sparrow." His answer was clipped.

"ETA, seventeen and a half minutes." Zillo's tone was similar.

Sam tapped the wristlet to disconnect the communication without saying goodbye. Seventeen and a half minutes.

That Zillinger idiot was some kind of tech god, and Sam understood that. But he hated it with every fiber of his being that he had to be the one and only person who could help get Sam back home. Why could it not have been someone else? **Anyone** else. Durand clearly trusted Zillinger. Sam, on the other hand, wasn't so sure that Zillinger's motives were as pure as Durand believed.

It had been hard to swallow his pride and accept Zillinger's help but he'd gulped it down anyways and been thankful for it. If this was the only way – he would have to deal with it. Deal with being in debt to someone he wanted to pretend didn't exist. The one he saw as competition, if he was willing to admit it.

The small rucksack near his feet was the only thing that he was taking with him. He didn't need anything, really. He planned to hit the ground running once he made it back, ramp the search into high gear, get everyone off their asses and out there. Wherever **there** was. He'd find it.

He checked the time, bent to grab the bag, and then began to make his way to the rear launch doors. The modified ship, a *Hypersonic*, that Zillinger was sending for him was due to arrive in less than four minutes. His Lieutenant, now helming *The Quentin*, was under strict orders to follow directions exactly as they had been given. A certain speed he was meant to maintain, a specific time when he needed get those doors open, and then another specific time when he knew to close them back up. It left Sam with very little time to make the transfer – to get himself inside the *Hypersonic*. There was zero room for error.

His breath was shallow inside his helmet, his heart pounded in his ears.

The siren wailed and he heard the metallic grinding of gears as the rear door began to ease open. He ran forward, only slightly hampered by the bulk of his suit. Standing on the lip of the open gate, ready to leap, he paused and scanned the vast open space ahead of him.

Where the hell was the ship?

CHAPTER SEVENTEEN

"That's a planet," River stated unnecessarily.

Both Zillo and Suki turned towards them. River returned their gaze, unblinking, nonplussed.

Suki looked back at the tiny speck on the old-time solar system map on display. "How could we have missed this?" she asked.

"Easy. It's not on any map; radar doesn't appear to pick up on it. It's possible there's some kind of natural cloaking." He shrugged. "Colloquially, it's called a ghost planet. It was, at some point in history, downgraded from planetary status. Likely, it had been explored but was not hospitable enough for humans. Eventually, map makers just stopped adding it in; no one had any reason to fly near it so it wasn't necessary. The planet was basically dead, a ghost," Zillo explained.

"That's… wild." Suki seemed lost for words.

Zillo was not. "I did some research. I was up all night. Back on Earth, eons ago, they had these things called newspapers. It was some sort of tangible news source. Many of them had been scanned and were just sitting there in The PRC archives. In 2005, the solar system consisted of nine planets. One year later, they 'demoted' one of those planets because it wasn't a proper size. I think that's what this is… that planet. Just completely forgotten. Well, until now I guess."

Suki moved closer again to the projection on the screen, reaching out her hand to touch what might have been a small smudge on the wall. *Could* Roxy be there, right now, waiting for rescue? Was it merely a coincidence that Seth Carmine was also nowhere to be found?

"You did it," Suki grinned, turning to Zillo. "You fucking did it!" She gave a whoop of joy and launched herself at him, laughing.

Zillo hugged her back, lifting her off her feet and swinging her around, her cane flying to the ground, before plunking her back down and shouting, "Look out, Pluto, here we come!"

CHAPTER EIGHTEEN

A low whistle pierced the silence inside his helmet, the only sound save for his ragged breaths. He turned to face the door, having retreated from its edge just moments earlier.

There it was: a sleek, streamlined, oval-shaped ship.

"You're late," Sam muttered out loud, then: "Great. Now I'm talking to inanimate objects."

The ship aligned itself with the lip of *The Quentin*. A door spiraled open on its side and there it hovered, waiting.

Sam braced himself and began to run.

And that was when the grinding began, the cogs and gears of the doors as they began to close up on him.

"Fuck!" Sam shouted and tried to run faster, his heart in his throat.

He couldn't blame his Lieutenant, Capaldi was simply following the orders he had been given, to close the gates when the countdown was over. It wasn't his fault the *Hypersonic* had been late getting there.

God damn it, Zillinger, Sam thought. *You did this on purpose.*

With one last final burst of speed, as the two gates began to close, Sam launched himself through the gap, pushing off from the claw-like edge of the door, praying he wouldn't be crushed between them. For a short moment he freefell into space, windmilling his arms, his legs spinning uselessly in place, before he landed, hard, against the side of the *Hypersonic*. Bent nearly double, he tumbled in through the small opening. His breath burst from him as he slammed against the console inside. The miniscule door – the one he had just barely fit through – rotated shut behind him. Before he had even had the chance to scrape himself off the floor, he felt a *whoosh* as the ship rapidly gained velocity. There were no windows in front of him but Sam felt the initial G-force slam into him and knew they were traveling at an extremely high rate of speed.

Within minutes the pressure surrounding Sam eased off, the ship having eased into some form of cruise control. Sam was now able to sit himself up, put himself to rights. With a gasp of pleasure he pulled the helmet from his head and took a deep breath of the stale but not unpleasant air inside the small cabin. He wiped the glisten of sweat from his brow, relieved to be safe and unharmed, glad he had managed to not shit his pants.

The *Hypersonic* was sleek but there were no extra bells and whistles. Sam had been told that this was merely a prototype, that Zillinger had rushed to finish it and make it space-worthy well before he had originally planned.

Sam was thankful. He absolutely was. But he hated it.

CHAPTER NINETEEN

"We're going to need more people," Suki stated, reading out from the notes Zillo had given her. "Pluto is approximately two thousand, three hundred and seventy-seven kilometers in size. How the hell are we going to cover that much distance on our own?"

"I'll call in a favor," Zillo interjected.

"How do you even have any favors left?" Suki snorted.

The three of them – Suki, Zillo, and River – had returned to Roxy's condo. Zillo had showered at the insistence of his friends, and changed into the spare clothes he kept at the office; they had convinced him to eat and drink something other than coffee and PWR Protein Delite™ bars.

They were now sipping spicy Adrak chai while they cultivated their plan of action.

"We need to narrow it down," River said, oblivious to having stated the obvious. "There must be a way."

"Durand will help," Zillo said. "He said he'd be in my debt, blah, blah, blah, after helping him out with the whole Sparrow thing."

Suki and River exchanged glances.

"How did that go?" Suki ventured.

Zillo glanced at his wristlet. "The *Hypersonic* should be reaching him... shortly."

"Why are you grinning?" Suki asked.

"No reason."

CHAPTER TWENTY

Roxy stood in front of *The Falcon's* cockpit console, her eyes gleaming with interest. This was old-school tech; so old, in fact, that she had only ever seen pictures of it on a Condo-Comm Interface screen. There were way more buttons and levers than were necessary by today's standards and it was at least twice the size of a Zip Ship control panel.

"What does all this stuff do?" Roxy asked.

As Brie launched into an explanation, Roxy ran her hands over the screens and instrument panels, now dark and useless.

"And this one," Brie concluded, "is the distress button. It sends a beacon. Normally, there would be someone monitoring from home base, keeping an eye out for this sort of thing…"

"I get it," Roxy said. "It's a shot in the dark."

"Quite literally," Brie replied. "We'd be sending a signal not knowing if anyone will ever see it."

"I know it's a risk but what other choice do we have? We cannot sit here and just freeze to death."

Brie nodded. "Okay. What's the plan?"

"It will come down to timing," Roxy explained. "We are currently running on what's left of the main power cells. There isn't much left in the reserves but it might be enough with the cryo-pods no longer leeching it."

Brie flinched.

"Sorry," Roxy apologized. "There's no way to make this any easier, I'm afraid." Then she continued: "How do we gain access to that reserve power so we can send the signal? We will need all the oomph we can get."

"We will need to turn everything off, flip the switches over to reserves. The main power cells will absorb the reserves. We'll give it a few minutes to fire up, then we turn everything on at once and hit the distress button," Brie explained. She paused and took a deep breath. "There will be zero power left after that, I am sure of it. We might have a day at most before things fully go to hell aboard this ship."

"Then we'd better hope it works," Roxy replied. "Where is the switch for the reserves? Not in here, I assume?"

"No, it's a failsafe, so it's tucked away. We don't want it turned on or off accidentally. Only a captain and the second-in-command would be aware of its location."

"We have to be careful," Roxy warned. "If there is an Abider on this ship, and chances are pretty good, I think, from the evidence we've found, we don't want them finding out about it. We need what's left in the reserves and we cannot afford to waste it."

Brie nodded. "When are we going to do this?"

"As soon as possible, I think," Roxy responded. "Maybe even–"

Roxy didn't get to finish her sentence.

There was a resounding boom and they were left in complete darkness.

***

They made their way gingerly out of the cockpit, not wanting to bump or knock into something important they would need to follow through with their plan. From far off, they could hear screams and an occasional dull thud.

"I can't see a damned thing," Roxy muttered, stumbling into a wall.

Brie grabbed her hand. "I know this ship like the back of my hand. Stay close."

Together, they ran, as quick as they dared, towards the trumpet of chaos.

And chaos it was.

Brie gasped as she entered the atrium, then began to cough. In the dim light she could make out the bodies that littered the floor, those who remained upright were coughing and crying; some were shouting, wandering around, not knowing where to go. An acrid smoke pervaded the air.

Roxy's eyes immediately began to water. "What the hell?" she managed to choke out.

"Has anyone seen where the fire is?" Brie shouted, trying to raise her voice loud enough to be heard over the commotion. She coughed. "Anyone?"

Roxy pulled her scarf over her nose and dove deeper into the room, searching for the source of the toxic vapors. She tripped – someone lay prone on the floor beside her. She knelt and felt for a pulse… nothing.

"We have to get everyone out of this room," Roxy shouted over the din. And then it came to her. "Brie! The bulkhead!"

Somehow, Brie heard her and began to herd those still able to walk on their own out of the room, sending them down the hall, shouting at them which way to go, what to do when they got there. With the scarf still tightly clenched to her face, Roxy felt around in front of her with her free hand, searching for those who had collapsed, searching for a sign of life.

She gave a shout of triumph when she felt a thready pulse and began to drag the prone person, one-handed, towards the direction she felt sure the door was in. Brie materialized beside her.

"The ones who could walk are helping those who can't; they're at the bulkhead. We've opened the hatch, there's some cool filtered air making its way in. It's freezing but…" She grabbed the other arm of the unconscious passenger Roxy was holding. "Let's get out of here."

They dragged the person out of the room between them, coughing and gagging as they went, their eyes watering so badly they could barely see, even when they were free of the worst of the fog. They slammed the doors of the atrium closed behind them.

Near the bulkhead, surrounded by others in much

the same state of distress, they tried to take controlled breaths, swiping at their eyes and noses in an attempt to clear them. The freezing air making its way inside was both agony and relief.

Brie tried to take a headcount. She searched the faces for her second-in-command.

The man they had pulled from the atrium, it turned out, was Jay. They'd checked him over. His breathing was shallow but steady, his pulse stronger now that he was near fresh air. He was lucky to be alive but likely to be ungrateful, given his well-known opinion of Roxy, when he came around and realized who had saved him.

"What the hell happened?" Brie addressed the group at large, her voice husky and raw. The passengers were in a sorry state, their faces streaked with soot, snot, and tears. "Who did this? Was it him?" She pointed at Jay, still unconscious on the floor, the most likely suspect amongst them.

"She told us all to meet in the atrium," a woman spoke up. "That you needed to speak with us again. We had no reason to disbelieve her. And then it was like a bomb went off and we couldn't see anything and we couldn't get out. Jay was the one who smashed through the doors, got them open."

"She?" Brie asked. "Who is she, Meredith?"

"It was Ingrid, Captain," Meredith replied between coughs. "Ingrid did this."

"That's not possible." Brie was barely able to get the words out. "I have known Ingrid Van Wyk my whole life, we studied together, were roommates at school..."

Roxy put a hand on her shoulder. "You should sit down."

"Where is Ingrid now?" Brie yelled, shrugging off Roxy's hand and stepping forward, fists clenched.

Meredith looked at her with a mixture of fear and pity. "She was in the atrium with us. And she didn't go back out."

Brie sank to the floor. "No, it can't be. Ingrid? An Abider?"

Roxy's vision had finally cleared. She started to count. She did it twice. Nineteen souls. Then a thought suddenly occurred to her and she counted again, weaving her way through the crowd, looking down, looking closely for someone small, and, finally, moving back to where Brie sat on the floor, her head in her hands.

"Brie." Roxy hated to even say it when Brie looked up at her, devastation already marring her face. "Victoria, the child... she isn't here. I've looked everywhere. I... I don't think she made it out."

CHAPTER TWENTY-ONE

Earth, 100 years ago (more or less)

There was so much to do to prepare. Not only were there physical tests to make sure that she was fit enough for this excursion, but there were also psychological tests as well. She had to be fit not only in body, but also of mind. Brie, of course, passed everything with flying colors, just as she knew she would. She was in tip-top shape.

It would have been difficult for most people to leave everything and everyone behind, to leave home knowing that you might never come back again. The decision was easy for Brie though... she wasn't leaving anything behind at all. Her parents were long gone and she had no siblings; she wasn't close to any other family, no cousins to speak of. There was no relationship, no husband or wife or partner to miss her. And her closest friend, well, she hoped to take her along for the ride.

The passengers had already been pre-selected: scientists, engineers, botanists, medical personnel, surgeons, tech experts. But Brie had been given free rein when it came to selecting the crew. She knew immediately who she wanted on her team. Dr. Ingrid Van Wyk had been her roommate through the entirety of her schooling. Ingrid's soft South African accent had been the first thing to put Brie at ease when she'd open the dorm room door, already overwhelmed with how big and bright everything was on her first day on campus.

"Welcome," Ingrid had said. "Looks like we're roomies. I am happy to meet you."

They were pleased to find, on their graduation day, that both had been selected to train at the prestigious IAB Space School. They'd rented an apartment, and did everything together. They'd drifted apart after graduation but had rekindled their friendship once they both found themselves working for The Relocation Board.

Brie picked up the phone and dialed the numbers she knew by heart.

"Hello," came the familiar tone. "Brie, how are you?"

"Hello, my friend, I am very well, thank you." Brie smiled into the phone. "What do you think sounds better, Ingrid? Doctor Major Van Wyk or Major Doctor Van Wyk?"

CHAPTER TWENTY-TWO

"Are we really going to do this?" Brie asked. Her eyes were filled with unshed tears.

"Take some deep breaths," Roxy told her, worried her friend was about to have a panic attack. "This will work. We have to think positively, that someone, somewhere out there is going to see this and come for us."

"How can you be so sure?"

Roxy smiled. "I have the best friends. I am certain, without a doubt, that they are out there searching for me right now. They **will** find us."

"And if they aren't looking, at the very second that we send this signal?" Brie asked, tears finally sliding down her face. "Then what?"

"They will. I trust Suki Kwan with my life," Roxy assured her, having already regaled Brie with tales of Suki and her misadventures.

"Isn't that the friend who's a terrible shot?" Brie sniffed, swiping at her nose.

Roxy laughed. "The one and only. Her aim may be off but her eyes are good, I assure you."

Brie took a deep breath and seemed to gather herself. "Shall we do this?"

***

Roxy and Brie went in opposite directions. Each would complete one final task before regrouping in the cockpit. If all went well, they would be ready to send a five second distress beacon out into the ether.

With the atrium now sealed, and out of commission due to the earlier explosion, the remaining crew and passengers, few though there were, had been sequestered in the hallway closest to the cockpit, where Brie could assure them, keep them updated, and surreptitiously keep a close eye on them. She wasn't sure she trusted any of them fully at this stage. They were subdued, for good reason, many of them still crying. They knew the risks but all agreed that this was the only way, their only opportunity for rescue.

It had been a lot to deal with: first a crash, then waking up not knowing where they were, the loss of their friends and fellow passengers, an explosion. They were lucky, though it didn't really feel that way. Many were mourning, and would be for a long time to come. Brie was mourning too and was worried for the souls she had been entrusted with. Roxy knew how she felt, in a way, had trauma in her past that she'd never fully dealt with. The best way Brie could help was to get these people the hell out of here. And Roxy was going to help her do it.

Deep in the bowels of the ship, Roxy had been tasked with shutting everything down. Flipping every single switch to the off position, disconnecting anything and everything that might be using a power source. Once that was done, she would rejoin Brie and they would set things in motion.

Brie had returned from the hatch secreted directly below where she now sat, had turned on the switch for the reserves and was sitting back in her chair nervously awaiting Roxy's return. She was taking deep breaths, reaching far down inside herself, searching for a modicum of calmness that she currently did not feel. She wiped sweaty palms down her thighs.

If this didn't work...

No, she told herself, *It **would** work.*

"It's done." Roxy let herself into the cockpit, closing the small entrance behind her, effectively cocooning herself and Brie within. It was quiet, save for the ragged, anxious breathing of the two women.

"Now we wait," Brie added, and began the countdown in her head.

They needed time to allow the power to drain back into the main reserves before they hit the switch.

Roxy grabbed Brie's hand. "We got this."

Brie attempted a smile, her lips trembling. "Thank you. I couldn't have done this without you."

"There's no other planet I would have wanted to crash on," Roxy replied.

The two women broke into fits of laughter. It was a relief to break the tension.

Brie's internal stopwatch had reached zero.

"It's time," she whispered.

"Together?" Roxy asked.

"Together," Brie replied.

Brie placed her hand on top of the large red button. Roxy placed hers on top of Brie's. And they pushed.

CHAPTER TWENTY-THREE

"How long is this going to take?"

"Patience, Commander, we will get there." The voice was thickly accented. "You will be safe with me. Please, stay right where you are."

Carmine sighed dramatically but crawled back beneath the heavy blanket under which he was concealed.

The *Roamer* who had picked him up from the parking lot had delivered him to an unknown location, after driving haphazardly for what felt like hours. Carmine knew their circuitous route was to throw off anyone who might be tailing them, though the possibility seemed ludicrous to him. As far as Carmine was concerned, his escape had gone off without a hitch.

It was uncomfortably hot and difficult to breathe huddled beneath the cheap synthetic wool blanket, in the back of a decrepit old Zip. The longer he had to lie there, the more incensed Carmine became. This was beneath him, god dammit.

He felt the Zip slow, stop, and then the low murmur of voices. Perhaps they were passing through some type of checkpoint. He forced himself to remain still; he held his breath and willed his heart to calm its heavy thud. If they searched the back of the Zip, he was screwed.

The voices continued for a short period and then the pilot of the Zip laughed heartily.

Come on, come on, you idiot, Carmine thought, *now is not the time to be making friends.*

The ship swayed slightly as if taking someone on board. Carmine went rigid.

Suddenly, the cool night air rushed over him as the blanket was pulled back. He squinted against the overhead light of the Zip.

"Who the hell are—"

He didn't get to finish his sentence. A hand was placed over his mouth.

He flinched at the sharp, cold pinch as something pierced the vein in his neck.

For a minute he felt like he was floating.

Then, nothing.

CHAPTER TWENTY-FOUR

"Durand has his team on it," Zillo announced, ending the animated call he'd just participated in. "The ones he can spare anyways: half of them are out on the search for Carmine."

"Good," Suki replied. "We're still going to do our own thing too, right?"

"Abso-fucking-lutely," River responded.

Zillo and Suki swung their heads toward River in shock.

"What?" River asked sincerely. "I learn things."

Chuckling, Zillo took command of CoCo. Typing efficiently on the air in front of the system, a satellite image soon occupied the far wall. "This is a live, in real time satellite feed," he informed them. "Let me get us a little closer. CoCo, please zoom to coordinates RA 20h 16m 15s | Dec -23° 2' 6" please."

"With pleasure, Mr. Zillinger," CoCo replied in a purr.

"Damn, Zillo," Suki laughed. "I think CoCo likes you."

Zillo blushed and rubbed a hand across the scruff

on his face; it was a permanent feature now, he had no time for shaving. "Okay, so if we all turn our attention to this," he said, changing the subject, walking closer to the projected image, "I have calculated that this is the most likely area in which we should search. Its current temperatures might allow human survival if conditions are right and if the person were to remain inside a properly equipped vessel."

"And if conditions are not right?" Suki asked.

"They have to be," Zillo replied. "I wish I could narrow it down further but I don't want to end up concentrating on the wrong spot and leaving everything else out. Durand's crew will spread out across these areas here." He pointed to several spots on the projection and they lit up with a red dot.

"I am surprised that you are not out there as well," River said. "A part of the search and rescue operation."

"I wanted to, believe me, but I didn't want to get in the way of the experts," Zillo replied.

Suki snorted. "If anyone is an expert here, it's you, Zillo. They wouldn't even know where to begin if it wasn't for you."

"I am of better use here, Suki, I can direct–"

"Is this where you want to be?" she asked. "Or would you rather be out there?" she said, gesturing towards the satellite image.

Zillo took a deep breath and sighed it out through his nose. "I think you know the answer to that, Suki."

"Then what the hell are you doing here? Go," she

yelled at him. "Get."

He looked at her, then looked at River. He swore under his breath and without saying another word, turned and left.

"Does that mean we're in charge now?" River asked with relish.

"We always were, my friend," Suki replied, holding her hand up for a high five. "We always were."

***

"Zillo just messaged. He's about to launch a second *Hypersonic*. He thinks he might even get there before Durand's team."

"He is a good man," River responded.

Suki was in the kitchen, rummaging through the cupboards. "Roxy never has anything good here. Where are the snacks? Where's the coffee? We'll have to order something."

"Suki dear," River said.

"We should get extra, in case we want snacks for later. And something for Roxy when she gets back."

"Perhaps you could come take a—" River tried again.

"Like, there isn't even a cookie or a box of crackers. She's going to be starving when she gets here, I bet."

"Suki!" River finally snarled.

Suki jumped, smacking the top of her head on a pantry door. "Fuck sakes, River, you scared the shit out of me. What do you want?"

"I want you to come and look at this," River replied, their eyes glued to the projected image of the wall. "Can you make this go backwards somehow, and have it play through again?"

"Why do you want—"

"Stop asking questions. Just do it."

"Jeez you're getting bossier," Suki admonished. "CoCo, replay thirty seconds of footage."

The screen quickly scrolled backwards as requested and began to replay.

"What did you see, River?" Suki asked, knowing the Mauwian's eyes were sharper than hers.

"I saw… **that**," they finally exclaimed, triumphant, pointing.

And then Suki saw it too. The flash on the screen. She ordered CoCo to replay once again and to freeze, to zoom and to log the exact coordinates. Then she screamed in excitement.

"Do you think that this is her?" River asked. "Is it possible? There cannot be two people out there, in the same area, sending out distress signals, can there?"

"It *has* to be her." Suki was grinning broadly, her cheeks flushed rosy red. "CoCo, video call Zillo."

"Suki, I was **just** talking to you," Zillo muttered, annoyed.

Suki and River could both see that he was suited up and about ready to step inside the small craft beside him, one foot poised on the opening of the ship.

"River saw a signal. On the satellite. It was quick but definitely there. I had CoCo pinpoint the coordinates and I am sending them to you right this second. It's her, Zillo, I can feel it. I knew she'd find a way to contact us. I knew it!"

"Are you fucking with me right now, Suki Kwan?" Zillo's voice was gruff with emotion.

"I wouldn't dream of it." Suki could not contain her excitement. "It's her, Zillo, it's really her."

"I'm leaving. Right now." He ended the call abruptly.

Suki cheered and threw her arms around River. "He's going to get our girl, River! She's coming home."

CHAPTER TWENTY-FIVE

This was taking longer than Sam had anticipated. *Hypersonic, my ass,* he thought.

He had dozed for a while, daydreamed, making plans in his head while he hurtled through space in a prototype ship built by a man who hated his guts. The feeling was mutual, yes, but that wasn't the point, Sam thought.

At first he had questioned if this might have been some kind of set up. A way, once and for all, for Zillinger to get him out of the picture, to have Roxy all to himself. But he kept going back to Durand. And if the Commander trusted Zillinger then, begrudgingly, Sam would have to as well. For the time being anyways.

Right now all he could think of was Roxy and where she might be. The possibilities were endless and he felt a panic course through his veins as he considered the vastness of the universe and all the many places she might be.

He urged the ship onward, as if by hoping, by sheer will, to rush it back to Aurora.

As if he had manifested it with his very thoughts, he caught a glimpse of light through the minimal porthole in the ship. It was merely a blur but it was more than he had seen for a very long time, days even, he suspected. He crossed his fingers that very soon, his feet would touch down on Aurora.

He would hit the ground running. It was time to get the show on the road.

***

Zillo strapped himself into the second *Hypersonic* prototype as the door spiraled closed behind him. This one had a few more bells and whistles than the one he had loaned to Durand for the Sparrow retrieval. He flipped a few switches, signaled to his ground crew to clear the launch pad, and once sure they were safely out of the way, hit the go button. A few short beeps emitted from the console and then he was slammed back into his seat with the force of the takeoff.

The coordinates sent to him by Suki had been pre-programmed into the ship's navigation system. Realistically, all Zillo had to do was sit back and wait.

It gave him time to think.

He hated having time to think.

He **wasn't** trying to be the hero, was he? He just wanted to find Roxy, to bring her back. From the very moment he had met her, Zillo had felt an inexplicable pull towards Roxy. He hadn't pushed, though he felt certain that she knew how he felt about her. And then Sparrow came back on the scene.

Roxy and Sparrow had history, a lot of unre-solved shit that Zillo feared had the potential to bring the two back together if they worked it all out. He'd accept it, of course, if that was what Roxy wanted, if being with Sam Sparrow would make her happy. He'd back off.

So, **was** he out here, speeding through space, hop-ing to rescue Roxy… so he'd have an in with her? So he could attempt to 'one up' Sparrow?

He settled back against the seat, judging himself and questioning his intentions.

***

The lights grew brighter outside and Sam was certain now that he was on fast approach to Aurora. Would he slow down for an easy landing or would he simply smash into the ground and hope he sur-vived the crash?

The instructions had been clear but brief: strap in and hold on.

He planned to do just that.

***

The steady drone of the *Hypersonic* had lulled Zillo into a restless sleep. He had worked steadily for days, both on the prototype for Sparrow and on the search for Roxy. He figured he could find time to sleep when everyone was home safe and sound. But it had finally caught up with him. His dreams were fractured, dark and confusing; they bordered on nightmares. Images filled his head of the missing Zip crushed beyond repair, of Roxy, hurt and bleeding, or worse.

He jolted awake to the sound of his wristlet relaying a recorded message. It was from Suki.

Sam just landed. He's safe. But also, kinda pissed.

Zillo couldn't help but chuckle. It wasn't a competition, intrinsically he knew that, but he'd take this as a win.

He wasn't able to respond to Suki's message; the rate of speed at which he was traveling did not allow for ease of movement. Suki Kwan was a force of nature but he was sure she would understand why he didn't reply.

He'd predicted how long it would take to reach the area the signal had come from and expected he should arrive there soon. It wasn't overly large, ideally it was made for one, but there would be enough space in the *Hypersonic*, and enough juice left in the tank, to get Roxy and himself back to Aurora. It would be a tight squeeze but he sure as hell wouldn't mind the tight quarters.

He planned a stop, grab, and get the hell out of dodge type of operation. He had no idea what condition he would find Roxy in; it was likely she would need immediate medical attention.

She was his sole focus.

***

The landing was rough but he had experienced much worse in his time. As soon as the vessel touched down, Sam dragged himself from within, falling to the ground outside of what looked like a large warehouse. He stumbled inside, finding himself in the glaring lights of CommsLink, greeted by the young woman on the front desk. The look of alarm on her face led him to believe he had not come through his arrival unscathed.

"Get me a *SkyShaw*," he rasped.

She didn't take her eyes off of him but did as he asked.

He hauled himself out of the protective suit he had been wearing, revealing his uniform underneath; much like himself, it had seen better days. When the *SkyShaw* arrived, to the great relief of the CommsLink administrator, Sam hurried outside and barked out Roxy's address at the driver, ignoring the curious looks that were shot his way.

He wiped a hand across his forehead, wincing at the brief pain he felt there. His fingers came away wet and sticky with blood.

It was a quick jaunt across the city. He ran past the security at the front with a wave, and then hammered on the door of the condo, barely able to contain himself. Suki Kwan's big eyes looked up at him through a crack in the door; he always forgot how tiny she was. He bent down and enveloped her in a hug.

"Glad to see you too, Sam," she grimaced. "No offense but you could totally use a shower right about now."

"Good to see you too." He couldn't help but grin. He was happy to be back on Aurora even if the circumstances were shit. He walked inside and spotted

River examining a projection on the wall.

"Ello my friend," River greeted him. "I am glad to see you have arrived safe and sound."

"What's this?" he asked, gesturing towards the projection. "And where's Zillinger?"

Suki and River exchanged a glance.

"What's going on?" Sam demanded, glancing back and forth between the two of them suspiciously.

Suki cleared her throat. "Well…"

CHAPTER TWENTY-SIX

Roxy and Brie sat anxiously, waiting. They both wondered how long they should hold on, to keep the faith, before they would have to accept the inevitable.

With no means of communication, they had no way of knowing if their distress signal had been successful, if it had been detected or seen. If rescue was on the way.

"How long before we give up hope?" Brie asked into the silence.

Roxy didn't think Brie expected an answer but she replied anyway: "We don't."

"I should go update the others."

"Are you okay to do that?" Roxy asked. "I can come with you, for backup, if you want?"

"No, I'm good I think, I think they'll be fine given the circumstances," Brie replied. "You stay here... just in case."

Roxy leaned back in her seat, wrapping her arms around herself, rubbing her shoulders hoping to create a bit of warmth. It was very cold on the ship now.

She felt sluggish. The liquid nutrient supplements were beginning to run out and they had, at best, a few days supply even with their dwindling numbers. Assuming they didn't freeze to death first.

She heard the cockpit door open behind her and Brie entered, her breath clouding the air in front of her face. "I told them not to give up, even though I don't entirely feel the same way myself. But it's my job to keep morale up, right?" Her laugh turned into a sob.

"Let's give it some time," Roxy reassured her, knowing that time was something they did not have a lot of.

Brie sat back in the captain's chair. She was the very picture of defeat.

"Listen," Roxy began.

The two women jumped at the boom that resonated through the ship. They heard screams from outside the door.

"Was that another explosion?" Brie yelled, her voice thick with fear.

"I don't think so," Roxy replied. "It felt like something collided with us."

That was when they heard what sounded like a knock.

***

Zillo felt the ship slow in increments, losing altitude, and surmised he must be reaching his destination. He hadn't removed his harness at all so was well prepared for a landing. He expected it might be rough – that was one of the wrinkles he hoped to iron out before officially launching this new tech to the world.

He felt a familiar thrill in his belly. The same one he got when something was finally coming together in the lab. He turned his head, trying to catch a glimpse of what might face him below.

He gasped.

From what little he could see, there appeared to be a very large ship resting on the surface of the planet. Even from this distance he could see it – it was listing, slightly on its side, long and tubular in shape. It looked ancient, the tech far less advanced than anything he had seen in his lifetime.

He could spot no sign of the Zip that Roxy had been piloting. The likelihood that it had been smashed to bits upon impact rushed fleetingly across his mind. He pushed the thought aside.

The *Hypersonic* slowed further and he felt the landing gear ease itself automatically into place. He was anxious to set down and get moving. He planned to dock close by, knowing the temperature outside would not be conducive to human survival for long. He would have to move fast. He prayed the suit would protect him, even for a brief moment, to get himself between ships. He thought he might be able to handle it for that long, and hoped he was right.

He landed with a heavy thump, his head whipped forward then back. He winced but didn't pause to take note of any injuries he might have incurred. The sound of the ship powering down spurred him on.

Quickly, he dispensed with his harness and pressed the button to release the lock on the porthole exit. Even in his protective gear, Zillo could feel the freezing temperature pressing in on him.

"Go, go, go," he muttered under his breath.

Finding no clearly marked entrance for the large ship in front of him, he did the only thing that he could think of and began rapping on its side as he moved along it, hoping someone inside might hear him. There was no point in shouting, he knew that, but he did it anyways, yelling Roxy's name over and over again.

His desperation grew, his movements lethargic, he began to slow as the cold began to leech into his suit.

With one last massive effort, he smashed his fist against the side of the ship.

And then, finally, someone knocked back.

***

"There's someone out there!" Roxy shouted, standing bolt upright.

"It fucking worked," Brie whispered to herself. She jumped to her feet next to Roxy. "Let's go."

The two women burst from the cockpit, weaving their way through the others gathered outside in the hall – they'd heard it too. Eager conversation followed Roxy and Brie as they ran past, heading for the access hatch on the side of *The Falcon*.

"With no power, this will be tough to open," Brie explained. "Put your back into it."

Together, using their shoulders for leverage, their legs braced against the opposite wall, Brie and Roxy, grunting and groaning, pushed with all their might. What little energy reserves they had left inside would soon be used up.

"Let me help."

They turned to see Jay standing behind them; the burly man who'd been so antagonistic towards them, was now striding forward. Purple bloomed beneath his eyes and across the bridge of his nose.

He leaned in beside Brie. She nodded at him and, together, the three of them gave a mighty push. The satisfying sound of the seal releasing greeted their ears and a rush of arctic air pushed inside. It was immediately followed by the crumpled shape of a man who tumbled in after it. Quickly, Brie, Roxy and Jay shoved the door closed.

The man on the floor, half-frozen, struggled to his feet.

"Zillo?" Roxy exclaimed.

"Roxy," he sighed with relief. "It's you."

"You know this person?" Brie asked, flabbergasted.

"I sure do." Roxy grinned widely and flung herself at Zillo. "Man, am I ever happy to see you." She hauled his helmet off, tossed it to one side and placed her hands on either side of his face before leaning in and kissing him soundly on the lips.

A strangled "Ditto," was all that Zillo could manage.

Suddenly, he was no longer cold.

CHAPTER TWENTY-SEVEN

"We have to get you out of here. I have already sent up a beacon from the *Hypersonic*. It's a constant stream so anyone nearby will pick up on it. A PRC crew is on the way, but..." he trailed off looking at the faces around him. He was clearly perplexed. "I think we're going to need a bigger ship."

"I can't leave," Roxy stated firmly. "I need to see this through, I need to see these people safely off this deathtrap before I go."

"Then we will wait together," Zillo said, equally resolute. He was not leaving Roxy now that he had found her.

Roxy gestured towards Brie. "Alexzander Zillinger, meet Brie Nova, Captain of *The Falcon*. Brie, meet my friend Zillo. He's one of the smartest guys I know."

"Ohhh," Brie nodded knowingly. "Nice to meet you, Mr. Zillinger. I'd shake your hand but I'm afraid my fingers might break off," she quipped.

"Likewise, Captain," Zillo replied, chuckling. "And it's Zillo, please." He wasn't sure in the dim light but he could have sworn that the Captain winked at Roxy.

Roxy began to explain, quickly, what had been happening since her Zip had gone down. The beeping her system had picked up on. How she had awakened on *The Falcon*. Their eventual loss of power, the unavoidable loss of life, the Abider who secreted herself aboard the ship and who had, in all likelihood, caused the initial crash. What they had sacrificed to send that one final signal. Roxy saw Brie out of the corner of her eye, how she had flinched at the mention of her former friend Ingrid. Roxy knew the events of the last little while would stay with them, with Brie especially, for a very long time.

"Holy fuck... an actual Seeker." Zillo's first response was shock, then, his eyes gleaming with interest, he glanced around the cockpit, taking in the switches and levels, his interest piqued despite their dire situation. He couldn't help himself.

"It seems almost impossible," Roxy replied, shivering. "Especially with survivors on board after all this time. I thought I was losing it at first."

"It's incredible," Zillo responded. "If I wasn't seeing it here right now, with my own two eyes, I am not sure I would believe it."

"One thing that still bothers me though," Roxy said. "Just where the hell are we?"

"It's a ghost planet," Zillo told them, confirming what they had already suspected. "It's not on any new solar system maps. We found it on some old Earth solar system documents. It's not an overly large planet but it's certainly not small. Thankfully, spotting your distress signal really helped us narrow down the search area. I left straightaway."

"You were right, Roxy," Brie said. "About sending out the signal."

"I know that doesn't make it any easier," Roxy replied, thinking of all the passengers who had been lost in the process.

"Everything else sort of fell into place after that," Zillo continued. "Thankfully the *Hypersonic* had been through pre-production already so I knew it was safe to use the prototype. We'd only used it for short journeys to test it but I felt confident it was up to the task."

"And thank goodness it was," Brie exclaimed. "I was really getting worried there for a minute."

Her cadence was light but Roxy knew that Brie had been through an emotional turmoil that she would not soon forget.

"Zillo, how is Suki dealing with all of this?" Roxy asked, already having an inkling of what the answer might be.

Zillo shook his head. "About as well as you would expect. All in, no breaks; she's a hard taskmaster, that one. But she gets the job done, no doubt about it. She pushed us all to the limits but I'm glad she did. Otherwise I'd have never found you here on Pluto."

"Wait… what did you just say?" Brie interrupted. "Pluto?"

"Yeah," Zillo responded. "That's where we are right now. The ghost planet. It wasn't easy to find but it does have a name: Pluto."

Brie looked incredulous. "I know Pluto. Well, I know **of** it. When I was a kid, we learned about it in school. My Very Excellent Mother Just Sent Us Nine Pizzas."

"Are you feeling alright, Brie?" Roxy asked, genuinely concerned for her friend's sanity.

Brie laughed. "It was a way for us to learn about all the planets in the solar system. My Very Excellent Mother Just Sent Us Nine Pizzas: Mercury, Venus, Earth, Mars, Jupiter, Saturn, Uranus, Neptune and Pluto," she explained.

Roxy and Zillo looked at her blankly.

"It made sense at the time," Brie finished. "They all still exist right?"

"Of course," Roxy assured her. "Everyone avoids Mars these days, 'cause of the dinosaurs."

Brie's jaw dropped and her eyes widened. "I'm sorry. Did you just say... **dinosaurs**?"

"Well, you see–" Zillo began.

"Wait," Roxy interjected. "Brie, we'll catch you up later. There's a lot of... it's going to be a lot. Things have really changed."

Brie nodded, still looking thoroughly confused.

"Do you hear that?" Roxy suddenly exclaimed, a distant whirring sound having reached her ears.

"It's a PRC Hover," Zillo replied, his voice animated. "They make a god awful racket but they get the job done. Sounds like more than one as well."

Brie came to her senses and let out a whoop of joy. The remaining passengers embraced each other, certain now that this long ordeal would soon be over, some began to cry. Even Jay looked emotional.

"Grab your things, only the important stuff that you can carry on your person. Photos and things like that," Brie advised. "Quickly now."

She turned to Roxy and Zillo once they had gone. "I wanted to give them something to keep them busy. Are we all assured safe passage off this ship?"

Roxy and Zillo exchanged a look.

"Of course," Zillo replied. "This is Roxy Buckles, she works for The PRC. You're safe with her."

If Roxy wasn't half-frozen, she would have blushed. "We can't forget Commander Durand either. He's a good person, Brie. You and your passengers will be granted asylum on Aurora until you decide what you want to do."

"We won't be returned to Earth?" Brie looked surprised, as if the thought had just occurred to her.

"You'd all be very welcome in New Cosmos," Roxy responded. "Unless… unless you wanted to go back to Earth."

"I have nothing left there," Brie replied. "Anyone and anything I had known there is gone by now. Too much time has passed. Leaving on this mission was meant to be my new start."

Roxy wrapped an arm around her shoulders. "It still can be."

The passengers began to trickle back to the hallway, chattering excitedly. They were eager to warm up, eat real food, and above all to stop worrying constantly about their own impending doom.

The whirring sound was getting closer, creating a downwash of air that buffeted the ship. Despite its large size, *The Falcon* swayed slightly from side to side.

A pounding on the outside, a replay of Zillo's arrival a short while ago, indicated the arrival of their rescuers from The PRC. They would have questions, no doubt, having expected to rescue one lone woman when, in reality, it was going to be a whole different ball game.

Together, Zillo, Roxy, and Jay wrestled the door open to admit The PRC officers. Their shock was almost comical.

They called for backup immediately, relaying the need for several more ships to fit all the remaining passengers in before they could be transported back to Aurora.

"We should go, Roxy," Zillo murmured softly. "Suki will be going out of her mind by now."

"Go," Brie encouraged. "We'll be fine now, thanks to you and your friend here. I'll find you once we get there or I'll make someone let you know once we reach Aurora."

"If... if you're sure?" Roxy was reluctant to leave now, wanting to see it through to the end.

Brie smiled. "I'm sure. If the stories you've told me about Suki are true, you need to get back there as soon as possible."

Roxy chuckled. "You did good, Captain." She reached for Brie and embraced her tightly. "I'll see you soon."

"Have a safe trip home, Roxy," she murmured, raising an amused eyebrow. "You and Zillo."

CHAPTER TWENTY-EIGHT

"It will just take a second to fire her up."

Zillo and Roxy were crammed side by side into the *Hypersonic*. It was a ship ideally made for one but Zillo wasn't leaving this planet without Roxy; had planned all along to bring her with him. The PRC team would be here for a while, checking on the passengers, waiting for backup, before they left to transport everyone back to New Cosmos.

The engine purred to life and a blast of warm air caressed Roxy's bruised face. She sighed in contentment. "I haven't been warm in what feels like forever."

"You can move closer if you like," Zillo suggested, suddenly feeling a little awkward but still glad he offered. "Body heat, you know."

Roxy grinned and closed the infinitesimal space that had still remained between them. "How long before we're back on Aurora?" she asked.

"Not long," Zillo replied as he flipped switches and pushed buttons. A deep vibration rippled through the ship. "We're about to take off, hold on."

It was nothing like flying in a Zip. Roxy was pinned back against Zillo by the force of the take off and, for a moment, until they leveled off, she wasn't able to speak. "Wow," she gasped when she was next able. "What is this thing?"

"It's my new prototype." He grinned proudly. "Cuts travel time by nearly three quarters."

"You really are the smartest person I know," Roxy responded, her eyes roving the inside of the *Hypersonic*. "Really though, Zillo, this is genius."

"It has come in handy. But I'm afraid you have River to thank for this rescue. They're the one who spotted the distress signal."

Roxy narrowed her eyes. "Only River to thank, hey? You had nothing to do with this whole thing?"

"I helped… a little. Suki too. Actually, she was relentless," Zillo replied, chuckling.

Roxy gave a bark of laughter. "Sounds about right."

"There's something else you should know as well," Zillo added reluctantly. "It's about Sam."

"What about him?" Roxy asked, her eyes narrowing as she looked at him. "He's gone."

Zillo looked away, fiddling with the switches on the console. "He was gone. So, there are actually two *Hypersonic* prototypes; this one I kept back for my own use. I allowed The PRC to use the second one. They wanted to bring Sam back to help with the search and rescue. The *Hypersonic* was sent out earlier today to collect him from *The Quentin*."

"Are you fucking serious?" She took a deep

breath. "The PRC wanted him back? I'm bloody well sure they did. He had absolutely nothing to do with it. Right. That man is insufferable."

Zillo couldn't help but laugh. "You're not wrong." Then he paused before saying, hesitantly: "But there's more, I'm afraid."

"Did he threaten you or something? Because if he did–"

"No, no," Zillo was quick to correct her. "Nothing to do with Sparrow. At least, not directly anyways."

"What are you talking about, Zillo?" Roxy asked, exasperated.

"Carmine."

The word hit the pit of Roxy's stomach with the force of a boulder. "What about Carmine?" she asked with gritted teeth.

Zillo took a deep breath. "We're not sure exactly, but what we do know is that he is not on *The Quentin*. It's been searched top to bottom. We are certain that Sparrow put him on the ship with the rest of the passengers – he was actually the first to walk on – but sometime between then and when the ship launched, someone else walked him back off. He's in the wind, Roxy, Carmine is gone."

Roxy's anger was palpable. "How did he manage to fuck this up?" she snarled.

Zillo felt a small twinge of satisfaction. "You're blaming this on Sparrow?"

"He had one job," Roxy stated. "And he didn't follow through."

She yawned then and her rage seemed to dissipate.

"When was the last time you slept?" Zillo asked her.

"Honestly," Roxy mused, "I'm not really sure."

"Why don't you try to grab a nap?" Zillo suggested. "You'll feel better after you get some sleep."

Roxy responded by closing her eyes and leaning back against the seat. It was difficult for Roxy to let go, to give in despite all that she had been through. But before long, her exhaustion overcame her, her breathing deepened and her head slumped over onto Zillo's shoulder. He adjusted himself so that his arm was around her and she was resting comfortably along his side.

He sighed contentedly and settled down for the rest of the journey, wishing, for the first time, that the *Hypersonic* didn't travel so damned fast.

CHAPTER TWENTY-NINE

"Are you fucking serious?" Sam was fuming.

River reached out a paw. "Calm down, Sam. Getting upset will not help."

"You don't need my help by the looks of it. Seems like Zillinger has everything under control," Sam replied, throwing his hands in the air. "He did this on purpose. He kept me away just long enough so he could rush in and save the day."

Suki rolled her eyes. "For fuck sake, Sam, get over it. You're acting like a child. I don't care if this hurts your ego or makes you feel like less of a man or some stupid shit like that. It's not about you. And dammit, it's not about Zillo either. This is about **Roxy**."

"She is right, Sam, my friend," River said. "We need to concentrate on getting Roxy home safely. This should be your concern as well."

He paced back and forth across the floor, hands on his head. He was vibrating with emotion.

"You're right. I'm sorry." Sam visibly deflated. "I'm being an ass."

"Understatement of the century," Suki muttered

under her breath. "But we're used to it by now."

Sam grinned, knowing that he had been forgiven or, at the very least, was on the way to being.

"Let's bring you up to date with what has been happening," River suggested, further attempting to keep the peace. "Suki, perhaps you can give Sam the details. I will make some tea."

Suki made Sam sit down because all the pacing was making her anxious. She explained how they had tracked down the ghost planet Pluto, how they had tried to narrow down the search area, and finally, the distress signal that River had picked up on, on the satellite feed. Suki made no attempt to downplay Zillo's contributions to the search and rescue.

"We couldn't have done it without him, Sam," she concluded. "I know you care very much about Roxy. Well, so does Zillo. We all do. We love her. It doesn't matter how it happened or who is out there doing the legwork. We're going to bring her home. That's final."

Sam sighed deeply as he accepted a steaming cup of tea from River. "Have there been any updates since he left?"

"Not yet," Suki replied, "But we didn't really expect to hear from him for a while. Right now we're just waiting."

"I hate waiting," River said.

They all nodded in agreement but there wasn't much else they could do. Silently, they sat, sipped their tea, and waited some more.

***

Roxy slept the whole way. Zillo dozed off himself for a short period, happy to have Roxy in his arms. He came around when the buzzer went off to indicate they were approaching their destination. He gently shook Roxy; her eyes blinked open and she seemed startled to find herself face to face with Zillo.

"You okay?" he asked.

"Yes, sorry," Roxy replied. "Just a bad dream. Where are we?"

"Nearing Aurora," Zillo told her. "It shouldn't be much longer."

"I... I'm feeling... a little..." Roxy slumped to one side and Zillo quickly grabbed for her to keep her upright.

"Roxy, Roxy, speak to me," Zillo demanded, shaking her.

But it was no use – Roxy was out cold.

***

The *Hypersonic* hadn't even powered down fully before Zillo was dragging Roxy out of the craft and onto the flight helipad at the Emergency Medical Center. He pulled the helmet off of her head, checked for a pulse – it was there, weak and thready; she was breathing, though it was shallow. He shouted for help.

Within seconds he was surrounded by medical personnel; Roxy was rushed inside. Zillo heard them shouting for a full body bio scan. He stepped out of his flight suit and threw it to one side before jogging inside behind them, keeping a close eye on the stretcher that held Roxy.

"You the partner?" a nurse asked.

Zillo hesitated for a moment, considering if the lie would be worth it, then nodded, afraid they'd keep him out of the loop otherwise. He didn't want to have to fight to find out what was going on.

"She's heading up for bio scanning right now. Follow me to the waiting area." She talked as she walked, Zillo trailing behind. She ushered him into a small room that looked like something out of an old Earth movie. "We will let you know as soon as we know."

He took a deep breath and reactivated his wristlet.

This was not a call he wanted to make.

CHAPTER THIRTY

When the wristlet on her arm buzzed with an incoming transmission, Suki nearly dropped the cup she'd been holding.

"It's Zillo," she shouted, in case anyone was in any doubt about who it might be. She tapped the wristlet to accept the call. "When did you get back? Where is she? How is she? Let me speak to her!"

"Slow down, Suki," Zillo replied softly. "We're here, we're in New Cosmos. Don't panic... but we're at the hospital. Roxy collapsed just before we landed so I redirected the *Hypersonic* and came straight here."

"What?" Suki shouted. "What's happened?"

"I'm not sure. She's gone for a bio scan at the moment. Get here as fast as you can. We're at the Center on Aethiopia Way."

Suki ended the call. "Let's go," she called to River and Sam. "Roxy is in the hospital."

"What—" River began.

"No time," Suki said, harried, as she hurried out the door as fast as she could with cane in tow.

With no other choice, Sam and River followed along behind, wondering what in the hell was going on.

***

Suki, Sam and River burst into the waiting area where Zillo had been sitting, twiddling his thumbs, ignoring his wristlet notifications and worrying, worrying and worrying.

"No word yet," he told them, seeing their frantic faces.

Both Suki and River embraced him, trying to convey their gratitude for bringing their friend home safely.

Sam approached Zillo and he tensed.

"Zillinger. Uh… thanks for getting me back here," Sam offered begrudgingly.

"Sure thing," Zillo responded in clipped tones.

River and Suki paced the confines of the room, tension and fear radiating off of them in waves.

A knock came to the door. Suki jumped.

The same nurse who had led Zillo to the room peeked around the door. "The doctor will be with you shortly." And then she was gone.

Shortly afterwards, a young doctor with light green skin entered the room. He was clearly of Witchlet descent, perhaps one of the young who'd not been eaten, who'd been taken in by a human family on Aurora. His face was serious.

"Which one of you is the partner?" he asked, his eyes roving around the room.

"Uh, that would be me," Zillo replied sheepishly, stepping forward. He saw, out of the corner of his eye, Sparrow's visceral reaction. "These are her friends. You can speak freely."

"She's got atypical pneumonia, a concussion; there are signs of malnutrition and dehydration as well. We would like to keep her for tonight, at least, for observation and treatment. She is currently still unconscious. Do you consent to the treatment of this for Ms. Buckles?"

Zillo looked to Suki for guidance. She nodded. He turned to the doctor. "I do. I consent."

"Thank you," the doctor replied. "I will have one of the porter-bots bring you to her room shortly."

He pulled the door shut behind him as he left.

Sparrow rounded on Zillo, his rage boiling over.

"Her partner?" he shouted.

"Sam, keep your voice down, this is a hospital," Suki admonished.

He continued without acknowledging her rebuke. "What game are you playing here, Zillinger? You're telling the doctors that you and Roxy are, what, married? Are you out of your fucking mind?"

Zillo sighed. "Calm yourself, Sparrow. I only told them that so they'd give me information on how she was doing. Otherwise I would have needed legal authorization for them to release it. This was much easier."

Sam was still fuming, his breath coming in quick gasps. His fists were held tight down by his side.

"Sam." River approached him, placing a paw on

his shoulder. "I know you are worried for Roxy right now, but you cannot take your anger out on Zingo. He did what he felt was best at the time. I believe, if you look past your jealousy, you will agree that this was the correct route to go."

"I'm not jealous," Sam countered.

Zillo gave a short bark of mirthless laughter.

"Shut your mouth, Zillinger."

"Enough!" Suki shouted. "You're being ridiculous and you're pissing me off. We need to focus on Roxy." And then she did something none of them expected... she started to cry.

For a minute, the other three stood there, stunned. Then they moved as one towards their friend; River embraced Suki, made purring sounds of comfort as they stroked her back.

"I'm getting your fur all wet." Suki sniffed against River's shoulder. She stepped back and swiped at her face. "Sorry."

"No apology necessary, Suki dear," River responded. "It has been... a lot."

Zillo stuck out his hand to Sam. "Truce? For now at least? Not asking you to like me, just to tolerate me for their sake, for Roxy's sake."

Sam stared at Zillo's hand for a minute and then reached out to clasp it. "Truce."

CHAPTER THIRTY-ONE

She felt like she was drifting on a warm, soft cloud. It was pleasant and comforting. The only complaint she had right now was that blasted incessant beeping noise. She groaned and tried to move a hand; it must be an alarm. She had to turn it off.

The problem was, her hand didn't seem to be co-operating. She groaned again and then heard someone speaking her name. It was coming from a distance. She struggled to swim up to the surface of wakefulness.

"Roxy? It's me. It's Suki. Can you hear me?"

Her eyes blinked open.

"Oh thank god," Suki breathed.

Roxy attempted to push herself up in bed, wincing. She looked at the many wires snaking their way out from beneath her hospital gown. "What the hell?" she murmured, her throat dry, her voice raspy.

"Ms. Buckles, glad to see that you are awake. Your partner and your friends have been very worried. I am Dr. Santorini. You are well on the way to being on the mend and, given the amount of helpers you have," he gestured to the full room, "I think you should be okay to go home in a day or two."

Roxy blinked in confusion at the doctor. He smiled and retreated out of the room with a small wave. Roxy searched the three expectant faces staring back at her.

"Sorry," Roxy croaked. "Whichever one of you is my partner, can you get me a drink? I'm absolutely parched."

***

"The doctor says it won't be permanent," Zillo whispered to the others as Roxy slept. "If her memory isn't back naturally by tomorrow, they'll administer the *Add-Mem* drug and that will speed things up, it will all come back to her within minutes. In the meantime, he told us not to give her too much information, they don't want to overwhelm her or make her upset. And, given that the staff think I'm her husband, we need to play along."

Sam glared at Zillo.

"Sorry, mate. It's out of my hands," Zillo replied, trying to hide his grin.

"Hey," came Roxy's hushed voice from behind them. She was awake. "What's everyone whispering about?"

"Nothing, babe," Zillo replied, swaggering to her side.

"He's enjoying this," Sam hissed to Suki. "Too much."

Suki turned to face him and spoke in a hushed

voice. "Look, Sam, I'm sorry if this upsets you, but Roxy **isn't** yours. I get that you're jealous of Zillo. But Roxy isn't your wife, or even your girlfriend, you're not even dating. Just… just tone it down, okay?"

Sam's mouth was set in a grim line. He said nothing, but he nodded briefly to Suki to let her know he understood.

Roxy cringed as she pushed herself stiffly up in bed. "You all look so familiar to me. Everything is a bit hazy but I'm sure it will come back eventually. What were your names again?" She reached for Zillo's hand, entwining her fingers with his.

"I'm going to head out," Sam interrupted. "Few things to do at The PRC. The whole escaped convict thing and all."

"It's Sam, right?" Roxy asked. "Thank you for coming."

"See you soon, Roxy," Sam muttered as he headed out the door.

Suki watched, knowing how much it had taken out of him to go.

"When can I get out of here?" Roxy wanted to know.

"Soon," River replied. "We have to wait until you are well enough."

"I think I'll be okay," Roxy responded, gazing up at Zillo. "This guy looks like he's strong enough to take care of me."

Zillo brushed Roxy's knuckles with his lips. "I'd be more than happy to take care of you."

"See," she remarked, her eyes shining. Then she

yawned.

"You should rest," Suki said.

"She's right," Zillo insisted, knowing Roxy would listen to her 'partner' before anyone else. "Let's tuck you in."

Roxy slid obligingly down in the bed, rested her head back against the starched white pillow, and Zillo tucked the covers in around her.

"See you in the morning," he said, leaning down to give her a hug, placing a lingering kiss on her forehead, breathing in the sweet scent of her hair. She was asleep before he'd even let go.

Together, Zillo, Suki and River left the medical center.

"Where would Sam have gone?" River wondered aloud.

"Probably exactly where he said he was going," Suki replied. "He's still got to find Seth Carmine, wherever the hell he is. And he'll be concerned over who the traitor is on *The Quentin.*"

"He's pretty angry," Zillo added unnecessarily.

"Yeah," Suki answered. "But he'll get over it. He needs to realize he has no right to stake a claim to Roxy like that. She wouldn't want that, I can guarantee it. No one **owns** Roxy Buckles. He shouldn't take it out on you either."

"Shall we head back to the condo and regroup?" River asked.

"You two go ahead," Zillo responded. "I might head into work as well, check over the *Hypersonics* now that they're back. See how they held up."

River and Suki climbed aboard a *SkyShaw* and Zillo waved as they took off into the skies of New Cosmos. Then he turned on his heel and went back to Roxy's room. He settled himself into the visitors chair in her room, propping his feet up on the end of her bed. In the morning, her memory would be returned to her. Until then, he wanted to savor these last few hours of having her as his wife.

CHAPTER THIRTY-TWO

The nurse came in just as Suntwin was kissing the horizon of New Cosmos. Zillo blinked himself awake, having stirred at the noise of someone else entering the room. Roxy slumbered on.

"I'm Ida." She smiled reassuringly at Zillo. "I'm just here to administer the *Add-Mem*. She will be back to herself in no time."

"Great, thank you," he murmured.

Zillo leaned back in the chair once the nurse had left and attempted to scrub the exhaustion from his face. He hadn't slept much that night, had been attuned to every movement, every breath and sigh that had come from Roxy in her sleep.

"Zillo?"

He dropped his hands from his face and rose from the chair to face Roxy. She was disheveled and bruised and clearly confused.

"What's going on?" she asked. "Have you been here all night?"

"No, no," he lied. "Just got here a little while ago."

"Why am I here? What happened?"

"You passed out," Zillo explained, "just before the *Hypersonic* landed on Aurora. I rushed us here to the medical center. You're being treated for pneumonia, a concussion, malnutrition and dehydration."

"I don't remember…" she trailed off.

"It's your concussion," Zillo explained. "Just some temporary memory issues that will have been resolved by now. It will all come back to you."

"Okay." Roxy nodded, then suddenly began pulling out the tubes and leads attached to her. With a swift movement, she tossed back her blankets and, cringing, swung her feet to the floor.

"Stop, Roxy, what in the world are you doing?"

"I have to find Brie, and the passengers from *The Falcon*, what happened to them? Where are they?" Her voice was frantic.

"Roxy, relax, I checked for you this morning. They're here, in this hospital, just on a different floor," Zillo assured her. "And they're fine. Everyone is going to be okay."

Visibly relieved, Roxy sank back against the bed. "When can I see Brie?"

"Let me see what I can do," Zillo told her. "Just sit back and hang on."

He returned a few minutes later. He wasn't alone.

"Roxy!" Brie exclaimed.

The two women hugged.

"You kinda look like shit." Brie laughed.

"You're not much better yourself, Captain."

Brie's short scarlet hair was a mess, it was completely flattened on one side, and sticking straight up on the other side. There were deep purple bruises beneath her eyes. But she was smiling.

Roxy sobered. "How is everyone doing?"

"As well as can be expected," Brie replied. "Thanks to your friend here, they'll soon have a place to call their own, once they're released from the hospital. That should happen in a day or two."

"What do you mean?" Roxy asked, looking between Brie and Zillo.

"It's not a big deal," Zillo responded.

"He's being modest," Brie insisted. "Mr. Zillinger here has offered free housing for the survivors of *The Falcon*. They've each been given an apartment in a building he owns, it's been set up for them completely with food and clothing and anything else they might need. He's even talking about getting them jobs. Once they're settled. He's a real hero."

"Anyone would do it," Zillo said modestly, a little embarrassed.

"They're letting me out of here once the doctor gives me the all clear," Brie told them. "I'd better head back to my room before he makes his rounds. I'll see you soon, Roxy, my friend. Glad to see you're doing well."

"You own an apartment building?" Roxy asked Zillo after Brie had left, surprised to learn this new fact.

Zillo chuckled. "I own a couple actually."

"A man of constant surprises, my husband," Roxy

quipped, giggling.

"You said... you said you didn't remember," Zillo stammered.

"It's coming back in bits and pieces," she teased. Then: "Can I go home now? Please."

"I think that can be arranged," Zillo told her. "Let me make a few calls."

CHAPTER THIRTY-THREE

The atmosphere at The PRC Plaza was frantic. Even more frantic than usual, which was saying something. Sam needed to keep his mind off of... things... and so here he was.

Alerts had been sent out to as far away as Earth, to any and all law enforcement groups to be on the lookout. So far, there was no sign of Seth Carmine on Aurora or off.

He would have needed help, and a lot of it, to pull this off, of that much Sam was sure. There were moles in The PRC and he wanted them out now, not later. He rapped his knuckles against the office door of Commander Hadrien Durand and waited. The door was opened swiftly by a large man wearing an earpiece and very large dark glasses.

"Yes?" he asked.

"Lieutenant Sam Sparrow for Commander Durand."

"Let him in, Singer," came a voice from the inside of the office.

"Sam," Durand stepped forward and held out his

hand. "Glad to see you arrived back safe and sound. That Zillinger man is quite the whiz."

"He's something alright," Sam muttered. "Any word on Carmine?"

"Afraid not," Durand replied reluctantly. "Unfortunately, he appears to have slipped through our fingers. We're still looking for him of course. We won't give up."

"I want in on this," Sam said.

"You are in on this," Durand told him.

"No," Sam insisted. "Fully. All in. I want this guy. I want to be the one to track him down and bring him in."

"That sounds like something Ms. Buckles would say." Durand smiled indulgently as he sat back down in the large chair behind the even larger desk that stretched across his office. Behind him was a large glass window with a spectacular view of New Cosmos. "Perhaps, Sam, you and Ms. Buckles might be able to work this case together? The best and the brightest that The PRC has to offer – I am confident that you will have him in custody in no time."

Sam goggled at him. "Are you serious?" he asked the Commander.

"Absolutely," came the response.

Sam nodded, easily warming to the idea. "Like partners," he said. "You can count on us, sir."

Durand tented his fingers and leaned back in his chair. "Let's make it happen, shall we?"

CHAPTER THIRTY-FOUR

Finally – peace and quiet. She very nearly had to beg for everyone to leave. Roxy had always enjoyed her alone time – she'd rarely had it over the last little while and she craved the opportunity to just **be**.

She took a long hot shower. She dried herself and slipped into an extra-oversized t-shirt that hit just above her knees. She ordered way too much food: baozi, cucumber salad, steamed dumplings, spring rolls, edamame, sauteed mushrooms, fish cake ramen, potstickers, kimchi pancakes, lo mein, egg drop soup, char siu pork, pickled vegetables, fried rice, wonton soup, crispy tofu and bok choy; and proceeded to stuff her face.

She had a very large glass of wine and asked CoCo to play some low-key music. She swayed to the melody and made her way to the glass wall to gaze out over New Cosmos. She sighed with pleasure.

And then the bell rang. A visitor.

"Who is it now, CoCo?" Roxy asked, not even attempting to keep the annoyance out of her voice. Whoever it was, she was sending them away. Promptly.

"Your potential guest is... Sam Sparrow," CoCo announced in her mellifluous tones.

"Oh, for fuck sake," Roxy muttered. Then, relenting, "Fine. Let him in."

Within minutes, Sam tapped lightly at the door and then came in without waiting for an answer.

"Roxy," he breathed, strolling to her and enveloping her in a hug.

Roxy returned the embrace. It was hard not to. It was Sam, after all. It went on for a little longer than what was considered conventionally acceptable but she didn't let go. Finally, Sam reluctantly moved back, though he kept his hands on her shoulders, peering into her face.

"Are you doing alright?" he asked, observing the bruises, the still healing split lip, her clean makeup-free face.

She met his gaze. "I'm okay."

"I was worried..." He broke off and stepped back from her as if realizing for the first time how close they were to one another.

"I know," she responded. "I remember you being at the hospital."

"You do?" Sam seemed surprised.

"Yes, it's all back now. Why didn't you stay?" she asked.

He seemed lost for words for a moment. "I didn't want to interfere. What with your husband there and all."

"Oh, Sam." Roxy shook her head.

"Sorry," he apologized. "That's not what I came

here for."

"What did you come here for?" Roxy asked, cocking her head to one side.

Sam cleared his throat. "I just came from Durand's office."

"Any updates on Carmine?" Roxy quickly asked. She tried to keep her voice even, to not betray the anger she had yet to let go of. Part of her still blamed Sam for this mess. Another part of her knew there was nothing he could have done. She promised herself she wouldn't bring it up. Not now, maybe not ever. No good would come of it.

"Unfortunately, no," Sam replied. "But, Roxy, Durand wants us to take the case. Me and you, to work together to bring him in. As partners."

"Seriously?" Roxy asked. "That's... that's..." She was lost for words.

"It's huge, I know," Sam finished for her. "It's the case of a lifetime. We will have a small team to help out with the menial tasks but, the two of us, we'll be feet on the ground, doing the legwork, tracking him down. Just like old times."

Roxy didn't say anything and Sam, all of a sudden, seemed a little less sure of himself.

"Oh," he rushed to add. "Unless... unless you don't want to do this with me? I'm sure Durand doesn't need us to be working together, we can probably–"

"Sam, stop," Roxy interjected. "Of course I want to do this. Of course I want to work with you. We used to talk about this, remember? Back at The Academy, what would it be like to work together on some huge, life-changing case?"

Sam smiled. "I sure do."

They both went quiet for a moment, lost in the past.

"Would you like a glass of wine? Or some food? I ordered way too much," Roxy offered. "It would be a shame for it to go to waste."

"Sure," Sam replied, never one to turn down a free meal or a free drink.

Together they sat on the couch, wine glasses in hand. Roxy suddenly remembered how little she was wearing and excused herself briefly to pull on some baggy lounge shorts.

They reminisced a little about old times, Sam asked her what had happened on *The Falcon*, listening intently and laughing when Roxy relayed the story of how she'd taken down Jay, the muscle-bound meathead who they'd all expected to have sabotaged the voyage.

"Instead," she explained, giggling "He turned out to be just a regular old asshole."

"Roxy," Sam ventured, his tone growing serious. "What's going on between you and—"

Roxy held up a hand to stop him. "I'm not ready to talk about this right now, Sam. I'm sorry but I need time."

He nodded. "You'll work this case with me though, right? We can do this, I'm confident we can get Carmine."

"Absolutely," Roxy replied with conviction. "If

anyone can do it, we can."

They said goodnight at the door, Sam pausing as if unsure what to do. What was the procedure here? How did you say goodnight to the love of your life, who you couldn't be with but wanted to, who'd just been missing, leaving you terrified out of your mind, but was now back safe and sound.

The wine had been a bad idea, Sam concluded and finally settled for bending down and kissing Roxy on the forehead before he walked away.

It was one of the hardest things he'd ever done.

CHAPTER THIRTY-FIVE

Roxy waved in acknowledgment at the girl on the front desk but didn't bother to stop as she made her way to the bank of elevators along the far wall of CommsLink. Stepping inside the first one to arrive, Roxy didn't push any of the buttons. Instead, she waited for the doors to close and spoke the words she had committed to memory: "Daedalus Lab."

The elevator began its slow descent, the walls flashing stunning imagery in an effort to alleviate the feeling of claustrophobia as the passenger inside traveled far underground. Roxy ignored it, choosing instead to stare straight ahead.

She hadn't seen Zillo since he'd sprung her from the hospital. She wanted to tell him in person that she was leaving to search for Carmine. That she'd be leaving with Sam.

At last, the doors swished open and Roxy stepped into the long, white, seemingly endless hallway filled with numbered doors along either side. She walked briskly, her heels tapping loudly on the stone floor, until she found the room she was looking for – number 144, Zillo's lab. Since the only way to access was Zillo's handprint, and Roxy didn't happen to have that with her, she stopped outside and rapped lightly on the door.

When no response came, Roxy knocked a little louder.

The door cracked open and Zillo's unsmiling face greeted her. It quickly spread with a grin. "Roxy!" he exclaimed.

"Hey, Zillo," she replied. "May I come in?"

"Yes, yes of course," he blustered, widening the gap in the door, inviting her in.

The lab was cluttered but not dirty. It appeared that Zillo had been working on something big; tools and large pieces of machinery littered the benches, even spreading across the floor. Roxy took a good look at Zillo – his hair was stuck up on end, likely from frequently running his hands through it in frustration. Several days of scruff covered his face. His shirt was covered in grease and ripped in more than a few places. His jeans were in much the same shape; Roxy saw bits of tanned, muscled leg peeking out through the holes. His feet were bare inside the scuffed sneakers.

"My eyes are up here, Roxy," Zillo chucked.

Roxy met those eyes. There were dark shadows beneath them but they were twinkling with humor. A different woman might have blushed.

"How are you feeling?" he asked sincerely, reaching out to brush his hand against her cheek but pulling it away quickly as if he'd thought better of the intimacy of the touch.

"I'm good," Roxy replied. "Some of the bruises have started to fade; I can move a little easier."

His eyes roved her face. "You look wonderful to me." He cleared his throat. "What brings you here today, Roxy? Not that I'm not glad to see you. I thought it was best to keep my distance for a bit."

She nodded. "You didn't have to though."

"I… I figured you might need some space."

"I appreciate that," Roxy responded. "But I need my friends around me too."

"Roxy," Zillo paused and ran a hand through his already disheveled hair. An odd look crossed his face, then he seemed to make a decision. "Roxy, I think you know that I want us to be more than friends. I've never hidden that from you but I don't want to push. Whatever is going on with you and Sam… I just think you need some time to figure things out without me being in the mix."

Roxy nodded sadly. "That's what I came here to tell you."

Zillo's face fell. He tried to hide it but failed. "You and Sam are back together?"

"No!" Roxy rushed to clarify. "No, not like that."

"Like what then?" Zillo asked, confused and a little frustrated.

"Durand has given the Carmine case to Sam and I," Roxy told him. "As PRC representatives, we'll head out with a small team, track him down and bring him in. We can't say no to this. It's a great opportunity. Commander Durand wants us to work on it, together, as partners. We leave tomorrow."

"I see," Zillo replied, rubbing at his scruffed chin.

"It's just work," Roxy assured him. "Nothing more."

"I know," Zillo said. "I'm happy for you. It's a big case. It will solidify your position in The PRC. I get that."

"I knew you would." Roxy smiled.

"I guess this is goodbye then," Zillo stated.

"Of course not," Roxy said. "I'll still be around, back and forth, checking things out on Aurora. There will be some travel involved for sure but I will always have time for my friends."

There was that word again: friends.

Zillo took a step closer to Roxy. They were mere inches apart. She watched him curiously. He reached out with one finger and tucked an errant strand of hair behind her ear, allowing his finger to brush down the side of her face and along her jawline. He ran his thumb across her chin, leaving it there, just below her lips. He looked up to meet her gaze.

"Zillo…" her voice was a mere whisper. "I'm not ready for this, for anything…"

"I know." His voice was low and husky. "I'm just saying goodbye."

He tilted her chin and slowly, taking his time in case she changed her mind, he brought his lips to hers. They were as soft as he remembered, full of promise. She didn't pull away and his heart soared.

From the moment he had first met Roxy at The Oasis he had wanted to do this, had thought of nothing else since that moment on *The Falcon* when she'd joyfully, yet all too briefly, kissed him.

He moved closer, molding her body to his and then pushed, walking her backwards until Roxy bumped up against the workbench behind her. He slid his hands down her back, cupped her ass, and easily lifted her so that she was sitting; he moved into the apex of her legs, pushing her skirt up, running one rough hand up her thigh. Roxy gasped but didn't stop him. Her fingers found their way beneath his shirt and he inhaled sharply as she ran her fingers lightly against his trim stomach, right above the waistband of his jeans. Roughly, he pressed against her, wanting to feel more of her, wanting less clothes between them. He caressed her face, moving his hands down to her shoulders and then lower still, groaning into her mouth as his thumbs were met with evidence that he wasn't alone in how he was feeling right now. Roxy arched her back, thrusting herself against the ministrations of his hands. He felt her reach for his belt buckle, was vaguely aware of her ripping it open, and going for the clasp of his jeans.

He put his hand on hers, reluctantly breaking the kiss; his breathing was ragged. So was Roxy's. He took a step back, reached out to pull her skirt back down over her legs, patting it in place, loath to stop touching her.

He didn't **want** to stop but he had to. For both their sake.

Her lips swollen from his kisses, her chest heaving; Zillo thought Roxy looked a little disappointed once he finally met her eyes. He couldn't help but feel a bit smug.

She slid down from the workbench, perplexed.

"Just a little something to remember me by... friend," Zillo said.

Roxy shook her head, chagrined. "Sorry, I got carried away, I don't want to lead anyone on, especially you."

"All good," Zillo assured her, still trying to calm his rapidly beating heart. "I get it."

"I should go," she said, walking back towards the door, her eyes still trained on him. "Bye, Zillo."

"Bye, Roxy," Zillo replied softly as the door clicked shut behind her.

He wondered how long it was reasonable to wait before he ran upstairs and grabbed a cold shower.

***

Roxy breezed through the door of *Buckles & Kwan Incorporated* to find a very harried Suki Kwan behind the front desk fielding calls, sorting messages and, in general, looking ready to murder the next person she saw who asked her to do something.

Keeping this in mind, Roxy skirted past her friend and the dirty looks being sent her way, and made for the security of her own office, easing the door shut behind her. She had a lot to think about.

The peace and quiet didn't last for long.

Suki stormed in a few short minutes later. "It's madness out there."

Roxy quirked an eyebrow in response.

"I know, I know," Suki lamented. "It's my own fault. But in my defense you were missing and you might have been dead and I was really worried and that took priority over everything else. There are a lot – and I mean a lot – of jobs backed up right now so I hope you're ready to get right back into the swing of things."

"About that…" Roxy began.

"Oh, no." Suki shook her finger at Roxy. "No, no, no. Do not do this to me again."

"I'm sorry, Suki, but this is big. Durand wants Sam and I to take on the Carmine case."

Suki's mouth dropped open. "Seriously?"

"Yes, seriously," Roxy replied. "We start today."

Suki groaned. "But what about…" she gestured to the front, "that mess out there?"

"Well, I think I might have a solution for that," Roxy said as the bell jangled to alert them that someone had come through the main entrance.

The two women turned at the sound.

"Ello," came a scratchy voice.

"Suki, meet Bareen, Elodie, Coben, and Jakota," Roxy said. "They have just arrived from Mauw and River assures me that they have the very best senses of their kind. I believe the term River used was **apex hunters**. They're going to give you a hand while I'm off hunting Carmine."

Suki stared around at the smiling feline faces in front of her, looking each one in the eye in turn before she grinned. "Let's get to work!"

CHAPTER THIRTY-SIX

It was a going away party of sorts, though the guest list was very limited.

Roxy was leaving in the morning with Sam, heading off on their mission to track down Seth Carmine. They had a solid tip that he had planned to hide out on Earth in one of the smaller countries. He'd be virtually unknown there, could start over from scratch, be a whole new person with a whole new identity.

The four of them gathered together, River and Suki on the couch; Brie lounged in a chair and Roxy was stretched out on the floor. She was surrounded by snacks; a bottle of wine (which she refused to share) sat next to her half-empty glass, which she kept refilling from the bottle. Roxy's time on *The Falcon*, surviving only on the nutrient liquid – she desperately wanted to put those days behind her.

Brie was thrilled to discover different foods; she too never wanted to see another nutrient beverage again. She loved her new home in Zillo's apartment building; soon she'd begin working at *Buckles & Kwan Incorporated*. Suki would need all the help she could get with Roxy off on another job and Brie wasn't ready to go back to her normal vocation quite yet – she would need a hell of a lot of training if she decided to. Things were a lot different here in the future. She was working through the ordeal that had happened aboard *The Falcon*, she had been matched with a trauma expert, engaging with them both one-on-one and then, in group therapy, with the rest of the passengers who had survived and been rescued. Even Jay seemed to have smartened up, never missing a session. None of them had wanted to return to Earth.

The four of them were avoiding heavy topics – for the time being anyways. They chatted about mundane stuff: clothes, food, books, the weather. They tried to bring Brie up to date on all the new things this new world would have to offer for her, things that did not exist back on Earth before she had left. It was overwhelming but she was handling it well.

Roxy's wristlet buzzed. She ignored it. It buzzed again. Sighing, she glanced at it and tapped the screen quickly to dismiss the message.

"Sam?" River asked, taking the opportunity to bring him up, ignoring the furious look Suki tossed in their direction.

"Yep," Roxy replied noncommittally.

"And?" Suki prodded, giving up all pretense, having decided she also wanted to know what was going on.

Sam had not handled things well, having arrived in time to merely witness the rescue, missing the chance to participate. He had taken it personally. Then the whole Zillo thing at the hospital – Suki was surprised Sam hadn't exploded from sheer rage.

"He's checking in to see if there is anything else that needs to be done before we leave tomorrow," Roxy said.

"That's not what River means and you know it," Suki retorted.

"Okay, fine. He knows I need time, that I'm not ready to jump into a relationship with anyone right now, maybe not even for a long time," Roxy replied. And then, knowing her friends wouldn't settle for just that, "It's the same thing I told Zillo."

"And we all know how that went," Brie remarked, chuckling. She shrugged and burst into laughter when Roxy shot her a look of warning.

Suki threw her hands up in the air. "Imagine! Having two hot guys lined up waiting for you, all you have to do is say the word and they come running. The horror of it all."

Roxy laughed at Suki's facial expression. "It's not as great as you would think, I'm afraid. And I seem to remember back at The Academy when you had Amber, Lexi, and Dimitri on the hook for–"

"Shut your mouth, Ms. Buckles, or I will start telling tales of my own," Suki responded with a guffaw, tossing a handful of Panipuri at Roxy.

"Who will you choose, Roxy dear?" River asked, cutting to the chase, doing away with the usual social niceties as they were often inclined to do.

They all looked at Roxy expectantly, waiting for

an answer.

Roxy paused for a moment. She smiled around at her friends. "You know what," she replied. "I think... I think that this time, I choose me."

ABOUT THE AUTHOR

Nicole Little lives in St. John's, Newfoundland. Her YA shared-universe novella, *The Lotus Fountain: A Slipstreamers Adventure*, was released by Engen Books in November 2020 and was shortlisted for the Write Project Book of the Year Award in the same year.

Invited, a horror novelette from Australian Publisher Black Hare Press, was released in July 2023 and Nicole's debut Science Fiction novel, *Roxy Buckles & the Flight of the Sparrow* was published by Engen Books in September 2023.

Her short stories have appeared in twenty-three anthologies. She has won several competitions including the June 2018 Kit Sora prize from Engen Books for her flash fiction piece "Sweet Sixteen;" her short story "Doxxed" placed 3rd in the WritersNL "A Nightmare on Water Street: Scary Story Reading" in October 2018 and her three-sentence horror story, "Tasty Babies" earned her the much-coveted Hell Hare award from Black Hare Press in January 2020.

www.ingramcontent.com/pod-product-compliance
Lightning Source LLC
Chambersburg PA
CBHW011429010726
47494CB00011B/2568